T0312622

AISLE NINE

AISLE NINE

APOCALYPSE ON SALE!

IAN X. CHO

HARPER
An Imprint of HarperCollinsPublishers

To my parents

Library of Congress Control Number: 2023947885

ISBN 978-0-06-320680-9

Typography by Julia Tyler

25 26 27 28 29 LBC 6 5 4 3 2

First Edition

CONTENTS

PART
ONE

BLACK FRIDAY IS COMING SOON!

SUNDOWN CITY

HERE FOR YOU MART

GET AN EXTRA DISCOUNT ON BLACK FRIDAY **20%**

Use this coupon for an additional 20% off your transaction!

VALID FOR
11/29/2024

Sundown City Here For You mart is a Relatively Safe Hell Zone. By visiting our establishment, you hereby acknowledge that the management is **not liable for injuries or deaths that might occur during your visit**. One coupon per customer.

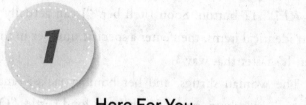

Here For You

A great smile can light up the world.

So says the packaging of the SmileBrite Whitening Strips on the conveyor belt of my checkout counter. I gaze at the old woman who placed this item on the belt. She smiles.

She holds up another box of whitening strips, then says, "A smile can light up the world, right?"

I smile back. "Sure it can. . . ."

As a clerk in the Here For You mart, I've learned that smiling really doesn't light up anything here. But it *does* have a function. In this dump, a fake smile is the armor I don whenever a customer hands me sweaty cash, or when someone thinks that the stock room is an Aladdin's cave, where out-of-stock items will magically appear if they only ask, "Are you sure you don't have more in the back?"

The old woman places dozens of SmileBrite boxes on my conveyor *one by one*. Her cart has hundreds of these boxes. She'll need to outlive Styrofoam in order to use them all.

Beep . . . beep . . .

My register becomes a metronome as I keep punching the *REPEAT* button. Soon I tell her, "I can actually count your identical items, then enter a specific number in the register. It's faster that way."

The woman shrugs, and her bomber jacket—made of hot-pink parachute material—makes a loud rustle. "Oh . . . I'm fine. But thanks for asking, *deary*."

In my experience, the worst shoppers are not the nutjobs or the "I wanna see a manager" types, but rather the folks who'll smile sweetly, chat politely, and then do whatever the fuck they want to do—and expect you to armor up and smile back.

"Nice weather today, eh?" she asks.

"Oh. It's lovely," I reply.

The forecast? Overhead halogen powerful enough to yellow plastic. Instrumental music that makes me feel like I'm trapped in a kitty litter commercial. Oh, and no AC above the checkouts because head office has decided to lower its carbon footprint *exactly* where I leave my actual footprint.

The woman grows bored and starts chucking the boxes on the belt at a speedy pace. I almost lose count.

"Ma'am . . . hold on." I hold out a hand.

I accidentally jab her shoulder . . . and freeze. Crap. I touched a shopper.

Our eyes meet. I stop breathing.

Suddenly she pokes me right back and winks.

I'm about to inch backward, but a distant warbling draws

my attention from the checkouts. I gaze in the direction of the sound: aisle nine. The aisle where a prison-style gate keeps out shoppers. From where I stand, I can see two armed guards moving.

A thud emerges from aisle nine. Followed by a deep howl. . . .

Working here, I've learned three essential things: First, as noted, the value of a fake smile. Second, the ability to withhold rage whenever someone mentions that the "Customer is always right." But above all, the importance of having good shoes—for all those hours I'm on my feet and for whenever I need to run from *demons* that emerge from a *hell portal* in aisle nine.

Aisle Nine

Aisle nine used to be homewares. But that was nearly two years ago, before portals to the underworld materialized all around the planet, all at once. Now aisle nine is a quarantined space with a "hell hole" that spews out a monster every few days or so.

I'm too far from the aisle nine gate to see any action, but I can hear flamethrowers firing up, and I shiver. But instead of a fight-or-flight response, I've got a fight-or-flight or carry-on-like-a-dumbass response—and it's terrifying that I take only about three seconds to choose to just carry on. Then again, everyone else makes the same choice, so maybe I'm not so special after all.

The SmileBrite woman puts more boxes on the conveyor but peeks furtively at aisle nine. "Say . . . is there something going on, um, *there*?" she asks.

No shit, lady.

"Oh, the team's just . . . busy at work," I reply, bobbing my head to the music.

The distant howls sharpen, and the woman and I move

faster to get her checked out. Behind her, a male shopper with a stubbly goatee and bad glasses abandons his cart and flees the store. The other folks in my line simply move to a checkout lane closer to aisle one. They're clearly worried, peering over their shoulders at odd intervals to make sure nothing comes crashing through, but they *refuse* to leave without our famous Unspecified Cheese Mix.

The howls . . . They're getting louder.

SmileBrite Lady swallows a lump, then says, "Maybe you were right. It's probably better if you just count everything in the cart."

I count the remaining boxes of whitening strips, punch in the number—*217!*—then process her payment. She pushes the bags of boxes into her cart, and soon she's heading through the exit. I'm obligated to announce every shopper's savings, so I yell out: "Ma'am! You saved *eighty-eight dollars* today at the Here For You mart! Thanks for coming!"

The next customer in line is a teen in a private school blazer, who barely looks up from her phone as she buys a mass of lip balm, and behind her is a redheaded guy getting a bag of chips. He seems almost eager to catch a glimpse of some demon-spawn violence.

"Busy day?" I ask the schoolgirl.

She doesn't acknowledge me, her gaze locked on her screen. She's holding it low enough that I glimpse a video of kids on a college campus. I wonder if she's trying to decide where she's headed next year. Unlike me. I'm just here, forever trying to decide the fastest way to check out twenty individual ChapSticks. The girl pays, grabs her things, and leaves—all without acknowledging my presence.

I'm about to ring up the redheaded guy, but before I can, he wanders away from the checkout and over to the aisle nine gate. "Sir?" I call out.

The in-store music gives way to a prerecorded message: *Thank you for shopping at the Sundown City Here For You mart. Did you know that thousands of* E. coli *bacterium can hide on the undersides of your shoes? Head to aisle eight to pick up today's super-discounted special: Sanit-Eze! Clean feet are happy feet!*

The music comes back on but not for long.

A gruff voice snaps over the PA:

"Attention, shoppers," our manager, Gully, calls out. "The store is temporarily closing. Please vacate immediately. . . ."

Translation: *Leave now or become monster chow.*

"*Oh!* While you're outside waiting for us to reopen, follow us on Facebook to get exclusive Here For You mart coupons!"

The remaining customers abandon their purchases wherever they're standing and leave without a fuss—except for the redheaded guy near aisle nine, who lets out an audible, angry huff as he heads to the doors.

I follow them to the front exit, lock it after the last customer has left, and then flip the OPEN sign to TEMPORARILY CLOSED. Now my job is to scan the store for stragglers. I start at the deli and then walk slowly alongside the aisles, checking them one by one.

Aisles one to two: Clothing and accessories. Basically, a polyester hellscape, where everything somehow smells deep-fried. Aisle three: Toys that also reek. Aisles four to six: Food with expiration dates that are strategically covered by *SPE-CIAL!* stickers. Aisle seven: Electronics. Smells surprisingly fine. Aisle eight: Hygiene stuff, but don't look up. There's a ceiling stain that reminds me of the poo emoji.

Sam is checking aisles ten to thirteen, while I hold my breath and stare at aisle nine. We're not supposed to go near here during attacks . . . but I find myself frozen a dozen steps away.

Before the world turned to shit, aisle nine would've held household crap—frying pans, place mats, single-serving coffee makers. Now? The space is sealed at its top and lined with padding that absorbs bullets and resists fire. I peer at the aisle's inner left wall and note that the middle of this section has a dark six-foot-wide circle of rippling oil-slick iridescence.

A portal to hell.

From what I can see, a furry pink orb of a creature has decided to pop out. It's the size of a volleyball and is attached to a silver chain that ends in a large metal hoop. I'm staring at an oversized pom-pom key-ring demon.

Damn. That's a *first*.

Was it a shopper who inspired this? Or a clerk? It's been theorized that demons are inspired by human nightmares and fears. But no one dwells on this too much because if it's true, it's impossible to control. I mean, *come on*, how are we all going to always have only happy thoughts in a hell-struck world? (In any case, nobody wants to hold up their hand and say, "Sorry! My bad! That pom-pom key-ring demon is from *my* nightmares.")

The nearest guard, Aaron Davis, aims his flamethrower at the beast, but the monster keeps ricocheting off the aisle walls and shedding pink fuzz. It's a hard target to center. Aaron is a squat, Hulkish dude, but fit as he is, he struggles to flame the monster while he's dodging its key-ring hoop. He lets out an *oof* when it slams into his chest and leaves a ding in his gray Kevlar armor.

Aaron wipes the fuzz off his helmet visor and calls out, "Ollie! Some help, buddy!"

I peer at the steel gate at the aisle's far end. Ollie Sheffield is waving his flamethrower at another pom-pom—a yellow one.

"Heard you the first time!" Ollie yells back.

A sinewy guy with freakishly large knuckles, Ollie maneuvers around the aisle and almost manages to use his flamethrower to barbecue the yellow pom-pom.

But then Ollie's flamethrower runs out of juice. He curses. Ollie drops his weapon, reaches for a long metal baton strapped to his back, pulls it out, swings, and smashes the monster into a wall. All this happens in a single motion.

The yellow pom-pom hisses. Rises back up.

With a *pop*, the beast sprouts two arms, two legs . . . and a *rabbit head*. It has bloodred eyes, pointy ears, and a ragged maw stuffed with sharp teeth. My attention swivels to Aaron's pink pom-pom on the other end of the aisle, as it too expands into a demon bunny form. Without warning, Aaron's rabbit spits out a sharp tooth . . .

That Aaron is barely able to duck.

The tooth shoots through the bars of the aisle nine gate, whizzes past *my ear*, and pierces through a pyramid mound of toilet paper. Heart pounding, I stagger away to find Norman and Dean doing price-check duty in aisle one.

We're not supposed to stop working unless a demon escapes aisle nine, and Norman and Dean work with an unwavering, bored calm. But as I move closer, I notice that they're not really working but listening to the action with breaths held. I can see the tremble in their hands. I know they're not only attempting to stay far, *far* away from aisle nine but also trying to pretend that nothing is wrong.

I'm happy to join them on the USS *Denial*.

But then Gully shoves me in the back. "Jasper! I've been yelling your fucking name for two minutes," he barks before ordering me to remember my shit, do something useful, and "man the fuckin' info counter."

"Right," I mumble as I head away, trying to ignore the sounds of battle. I sit behind the info counter and furtively check my watch. Forty-five minutes till the end of my shift.

Forty-four minutes and thirty seconds, to be precise. . . .

A phone beside me rings. I pick it up. "Here For You mart. Jasper speaking. How may I assist you?"

"Do you folks sell the inserts for a hot-water bottle?" says a guy.

"Inserts? You mean, *hot water*?" I reply.

"*Yeah.* You people sell chilled bottled water and bags of ice, right? What about fresh hot water?"

Suddenly I hear a rumble in front of me, and I peer over the counter's edge, knowing instantly just what I'm about to find.

"Hello . . . ?" says the man on the phone.

I lower the receiver and realize I'm staring at a *third* bunny key-ring demon—this one pale blue. Somehow, it's managed to slip out past the gates. I don't dare breathe. I back away from the counter's edge and reach for a nearby intercom.

"Uh, guys," I announce in a whisper that the whole store can hear, "could I get some . . . um . . . pricing help on a fuzzy blue demon at the info counter?"

No reply.

The *ON* light on the intercom unit isn't lit up. I fiddle with the switches but can't get it activated.

Great.

I reach into a drawer for a hammer and take it out slowly, soundlessly.

Judging by a nearby rumble, the creature is standing below but right in front of the info counter. I take two steps back and then make a break for the exit doors . . . only to remember that they're locked.

Shit. I realize I've left the keys somewhere, that I'm trapped.

A growl echoes behind me, and in a door's reflection I see the blue rabbit bounding toward me. I spin around. The demon bunny has stopped a yard away. It snarls and stands on its hind legs. Its eyes glow red.

The bunny sniffs the air. Tips its head to the side.

No sudden moves, I tell myself. But my feet don't listen. I stumble backward, my shoulders slamming against the glass doors. The bunny growls and reaches behind itself. I hear a creaking as it unlatches the key chain from its back. The rabbit twirls its chain like a lasso. It seems ready to end my seventeen-year stint on the planet.

I tell myself to lift my hammer—

Then realize I left it at the counter.

"This *cannot* be happening."

Footsteps echo up ahead.

The monster halts, then turns toward the sound. Kyle Kuan is racing through the checkout aisles. Her highlighter-yellow hair flips up like a halo against the fluorescent lights. She's got a flamethrower on a crossbody strap, and her Kevlar vest has the yellow words *VANGUARD MILITARY*.

Like me, Kyle's just seventeen. But unlike me, she seems to know exactly what the fuck she's doing.

Kyle dons her trainee-guard helmet, grips her flame-thrower, then steps up to the rabbit demon. Her finger twitches on the trigger. The demon bristles. A plastic bag drifts by like a tumbleweed. Abruptly, the monster rushes toward her, and Kyle raises her flamethrower and fires a golden burst into the air.

The rabbit's fur singes, and it scuttles back, throws its key ring at Kyle.

"Look out!" I yell.

Kyle ducks. She adjusts her flamethrower to focus her fire into a narrow, longer beam to strike the rabbit from a greater distance. The air stinks of melted plastic fur. The demon tries to revert to a pom-pom but fails. With a yelp, it crawls half-dead into a nearby instant photo booth.

Kyle turns off her flamethrower and enters the booth. I move closer to watch in awe. Through a gap in the curtain, I see her bludgeoning the limp bunny with her gun's butt. On the backswing, Kyle accidentally bumps the photo booth controls, and the machine emits a flash. I barely hear the *click* amid all the violent whacking. Two flashes later, the beast is a lifeless meat sack.

Kyle huffs, flops exhausted onto the booth stool, and takes off her helmet—and I can't help but wish I were the camera's red light so I could be in there with her. I'm literally *envious* of a bulb.

Her eyeline rises, and I think she's staring at the booth's preview screen. She catches a breath, blows her bangs off her forehead.

The machine lets out a final flash. *Click.*

Kyle pulls out a dagger, skewers it into the demon-rabbit carcass, and carries the body out of the photo booth. As she wanders off, I realize the booth is beeping—a photo is ready—so I reach into my pocket for a coin.

Soon I'm holding a photo strip.

The first three pictures show Kyle pulping the monster, each frame bloodier than the one before. However, the last frame is the most startling: Kyle, battle angel, gazing into the camera like she's staring back at me with her piercing jet-black eyes.

"Hey!" I call out to Kyle. "Thanks for the save!"

Kyle pauses to peer over her shoulder. She shoots me a look that suggests she's annoyed that I stumbled (yet again) into a near-fatal demon encounter. Last week, I got too close to aisle nine when a porcupine demon was shooting spikes; I would've become a human pincushion if Kyle hadn't saved me.

But even though her stare conveys aggravation, I still get a burst of euphoria and giddy hopefulness. Anytime Kyle looks my way—even if it's for all the wrong reasons—I'm like a fly pulled toward the deli's UV lamp.

Before I know it, Kyle's headed over to aisle nine, where Aaron and Ollie have slain their own demon rabbits. The quarantine gate has been opened, and Kyle starts helping the guys dispose of the carcasses.

My breathing slows until I look at the ground to see demon blood drying in a way that looks like . . . letters of the alphabet: *h i*

"What the hell?" I mumble.

Banging sounds echo in, and I turn to see shoppers knocking impatiently on the glass doors as they wait for the mart to reopen. I flick my gaze back to the blood, only to find the eerie globs are now just innocuous shapes.

Unlike the bargain-hunting beasts waiting outside.

3

A Strange New Normal

On Christmas Day almost two years ago, thousands upon thousands of hell portals opened simultaneously across the world. They appeared in random places: From famous spots—Buckingham Palace, George Washington's left eye on Mount Rushmore—to ordinary spaces like classrooms, homes, and KFCs. Nearly sixty thousand portals appeared in North America alone.

That day, about 1 percent of all portals spewed monsters. Phantasmagoric beasts, the likes of which the world had never seen before, spilled out into streets, offices, homes. Most of those active portal spots became bloodbaths. But eventually, the world's militaries managed to slay the demons and hold back subsequent incursions.

So, Hell Portal Day wasn't an apocalypse per se.

But the confirmed existence of Satan's kingdom led to a shitstorm of chaos. It caused looting, murders, suicides, mass baptisms. YouTube became an unmoderated snuff video channel before it threw up a *404 Error* message itself. Cults sprung up like weeds in the wake of all the fear and hopelessness.

Governments strained to fight demons and hold back anarchy.

Then the Vanguard Corporation stepped up.

Vanguard is a mega-conglomerate that specialized in billion-dollar weapon and surveillance systems long before Hell Portal Day. In the midst of all the chaos, Vanguard offered to bring back *normality*. With everything falling apart, and everyone lost in despair, it didn't take long for the president of the United States to accept their help.

Within weeks, the Vanguard Corporation had quarantined all of America's portals. They rolled out private military forces—armed with the latest tech—to every city. They broadcast their wins all over social media and turned soldiers into heroes we all could believe in. Oh, and they helped little old ladies safely cross the street to access newly reopened Walmarts and Costcos.

From there, Vanguard went on to protect the entire western world. Countries gave the corporation more and more authority to do whatever it deemed necessary to keep people safe. Sure, you hear the occasional rumbling about "corpo-martial law" but it's easy to ignore those concerns. (Just google the countries that refused Vanguard's help, and you'll find whole towns that were *digested* by demons.) Eventually, Vanguard set their spin machine on the general public—and started pushing the idea that life in a portal-riddled world was still highly *livable*.

And as it turned out, civilians learned pretty quickly to just . . . carry on.

People resumed carpooling their kids to soccer practice.

They went back to swiping left and right. They fought, screwed, abused each other, and wept about their messy lives. They watched *Dr. Phil*. All in all, it seemed most of us were happy to tolerate a strange new normal as long as we didn't have to look too closely at the strangeness.

But these days, looking closely is all I seem to do. . . .

As I walk home from work, I gaze around at the businesspeople, FedEx couriers, and busy, bustling parents. There are no portals in the immediate area, just tall gray buildings and warm breezes. Everyone moves with a surprising calm. But still, I'm never quite sure how safe we really are: there's *always* Vanguard patrolmen stalking up and down the sidewalks, the sound of their boots setting the tempo for the city.

To my right, two Vanguard workers are plastering up posters of Lady Gaga. She's got a speech bubble over her head that reads: "Hey there! Install the Vanguard app to receive alerts about No-Go Zones. Stay safe and live your best life!"

The edge of the poster reads, "Vanguard thanks you for reading this message. Please open the app to receive one complimentary VC point!"

I pull out my phone, open the Vanguard app, and a microchip embedded in the poster causes my device to make a coin-clink sound. My Vanguard account has been credited with one VC point. (Each week I usually snare about seventy points—enough to redeem a free Baskin-Robbins single-scoop cone.) I pass a barbershop called Close Cuts, and the same app flashes with the message: **Close Cuts is a Relatively**

Safe Hell Zone that has one portal. Pausing to peer in the window, I'm instantly gifted a half-off coupon.

No surprise, the barbershop is packed.

During the first ninety days of its mission to fix America, Vanguard instituted huge lockdowns to allow them to repair cities and relocate people from the worst danger zones. But when the lockdowns ended and the repairs were done, Vanguard was unwilling to turn every portal-riddled workplace into a No-Go Zone.

To protect the economy, Vanguard identified workspaces that contained "relatively low-risk portals" and allowed bosses and staff there to keep on keeping on. In fact, they *encouraged* this by offering hazard pay and increased benefits. The downside of working in a low-risk zone? Nothing big . . . aside from the constant risk of a painful, monster-related death.

"Yo!" a voice calls out.

I've dawdled in a crosswalk, and a VC patrolman tells me to keep moving. I start walking again, and a glare of afternoon light hits me in the face. I shield my eyes. Through my fingers, the reddish light almost makes it look as though the building tops are on fire.

My pulse speeds up.

I lower my gaze to see the world clearly again.

Everything's fine. Just keep moving, Jasper. . . .

I enter my apartment building and take the stairs up to my place, but when I round the corner, I find a Pizza Hut delivery guy kneeling in front of my door. He's trying to push slices of a pepperoni pizza through the gap by the floor.

A female voice emerges from inside: "Keep going! Don't worry if toppings fall off."

Great. Lara has ordered pizza, and now that I'm here, I'm going to have to tip the guy. I give him the loose change in my pocket, then watch him head for the elevator bank, disgusted.

As soon as he's out of sight, I open my apartment door and slip inside. The carpeting is covered in grease and cheese, but my gaze soon focuses on a stuffed toy—a white-furred plush kitty—sitting on the sofa, chowing down on a ruined-looking slice of pizza.

"Lara!"

The plush cat looks up at me. "Oh, hey, Jasper. How was your day?" she asks.

"Lara, that's disgusting." I shut the door. "You know you're not supposed to eat food off the floor."

She laughs. "Yeah, that doesn't really apply to me, does it?"

Right. Lara probably isn't capable of getting food poisoning, since she's not even of this world. She's a demon inspired by some person's fear of stuffed animals or cats or, who knows, maybe both.

She came to live with me about three months ago. I'd left a window open, and she wandered in. At first, I thought she was a stray, but when I went to pet her, I noticed her plastic eyes and toy stitch lines. And I freaked.

But then Lara held out a paw and said, "Hey! Don't be scared! I'm not gonna hurt you!"

Her voice sounded like something from a cartoon, and her overpowering *cuteness* held me back. "You can . . . talk?" I asked, inching closer. I'd never heard of demons talking.

"Look, I won't hurt you. I just need a place to hide from—" Lara paused to look out the window. I could see a small squad of Vanguard soldiers massing on the corner. Not good. But then she spotted a small box of pizza in my hand. I'd forgotten I was holding it. She took a sniff, her eyes widening. "What . . . is . . . *that*?"

"Pizza?"

I pulled out a slice and held it out to her. She took a bite and then released an enormous purr. It was the sweetest sound I'd ever heard.

"Look, I promise I'm not here to harm you," Lara said. "I just need a place to crash." It turned out she was one of a *very* small number of demons that had managed to avoid being killed by Vanguard. But all she wanted was to never have to go back to hell. She didn't want to cause anyone any harm.

Now, here's the thing—the new laws state that if you encounter unexpected demons, you're supposed to summon assistance on your Vanguard app immediately. And it's a helluva lot of VC points if you're the *first* to call in a stray demon.

But then, Lara reached out to place a soft paw on my knee. Without thinking, I gingerly rubbed the plastic fur on her neck, and well, you know what they say: cats choose their humans.

It's been months since that day. She's a pretty chill roomie, but I still don't know anything about her life in hell. Whenever I pry, she *always* tries to downplay the underworld—"There's not much to talk about"—as though it's just a bad neighborhood full of loser exes she'd rather forget.

Obviously, Lara's got secrets. But I like living with her: all she *ever* wants to do is watch TV, eat fast food, and hang out . . . which pretty much makes her my best friend.

"Want some pizza?" she asks.

I stare at the greasy floor. "Lara. You do know that messes like this make it *impossible* for me to ever have company over, right?"

"Ha! And who exactly were you planning to invite?" she asks matter-of-factly. "If it wasn't for me, you know you'd be eating all by yourself."

Ouch. Lara's sewn-on tag—the one that reads *100% POLYESTER*—should also state, *0% FILTER*.

I reach down to pet her. "Love you too, buddy."

Lara shoots me a smile that would make a Disney animator jealous.

After dinner, while I'm toweling myself dry from a shower, Lara knocks on the bathroom door and says, "Hey. I need to use the toilet."

"Out in a sec," I reply. "But you know, you can always use the litter box."

She hisses. "I'm gonna pretend you didn't say that."

Lara wanders off, and as I change into my pajamas, I

notice myself in the bathroom mirror. With my finger, I trace the length of the mean-looking scar that runs from the middle of my hairline to my left eyebrow like a serpent's tail.

It's been five months since *the accident*. It was so stupid. I was price-checking in aisle three when a hanging, hard-plastic piggy bank decoration thing fell on my head. I awoke in the hospital, my head in a helmet of bandages.

Ever since, whenever I look at myself in the mirror, I feel like a stranger in my own body. All I see is this reedy young guy with floppy dark hair and darker eyes—and I always need to remind myself: that's *me*. It's why sometimes Gully can yell my name and I don't know who he's talking to until he comes up and pokes me.

My head trauma certainly did a number on me. I still remember shit, like general knowledge about the world, portals, retail, YouTube memes. But the section of my brain that holds actual *personal memories*—of my life and experiences from before the accident—is entirely blank. I have no past. Honestly, if it weren't for a nurse telling me about my accident, I wouldn't even *know* how I wound up in a hospital bed.

"Who are you?" I ask my reflection.

I wander through my tiny apartment—well, technically my parents' place—and take in the things I can observe. It's like being in a museum but without labels. Over in the living room, the pictures on the wall show two parents and an only child: *me*.

My mom seemed to favor fringed skirts and oversized

wood-bead jewelry. My dad always seemed to be stretching his smile as big as possible. In one picture, at the beach, he's got on a T-shirt that reads *You Cat to Be Kitten Me!* And I have this feeling that if he were a piñata, he'd release cheesy dad jokes instead of candy when you whacked him open. But I don't actually remember anything about them. They might as well be *strangers*.

I stare closer at that beach pic—the way my dad rests his hand on my shoulder, the way my mom seems to be sneaking a peek at me—and I like to believe our family was super close. But that's just one of a hundred assumptions I've made about my life before hell opened up.

Problem is that I can't just ask my parents. According to an obituary I found in a drawer, they both died on Hell Portal Day. There's not a lot of info in the clipping, but there are some deep claw marks on the ground level of my apartment building—

I shudder. I refuse to let my thoughts go there.

Instead, I try to piece *myself* together from tidbits of info I can gather in my apartment. On the doorframe, someone used a Sharpie to mark my height from toddler to age thirteen. In the hall, there's a closet with old knickknacks; in the living room, a bookshelf packed with sci-fi books; and in my bedroom, a desk with a homemade diorama of the *Return of the Jedi* Ewok village.

(I recently discovered I can list every Ewok ever mentioned in the Star Wars universe, in *alphabetical* order—*Chief*

Chirpa . . . Chubbray . . . Flitchee . . .—which *does* paint a pretty good picture, I suppose, of the kid I was.)

No one's bothered to check in on me over these past five months, but I keep thinking wishfully—all right, *deludedly*—that I've got a friend who's out there trying desperately to get in touch. Of course, I could learn a whole lot more about my past social life if I could check my laptop and old phone, get onto my social media accounts, answer some emails. But I don't remember any passwords. FML.

I slump onto my bed and stare at the ceiling and walls. Surfaces that have nothing but Blu Tack dots. When I first came home from the hospital, I figured the dots had once held up posters. But then I opened a bedside drawer to find a large photo . . . of a street dumpster graffitied with the words *No place like home* and filled with flaming garbage. On the ground in front of the dumpster are the shadows of two people: what looks like a guy holding out a phone to take this picture, and a girl holding his hand.

I can't tell if it's *my* shadow in the pic. Maybe it's just a quirky image I printed off Instagram. But the back of this photo has Blu Tack stains, which always makes me wonder: *Was my bedroom once wallpapered in weird photos like this?*

And damn, was there a girl in all of them?

I stare at those two figures and try to dig out a memory of a girlfriend and a burning dumpster. But . . . nada. Squeezing my eyes shut, I try to pull out a lost memory of *anything*—friends, family, someone, anyone from my past.

But barely seconds later, a sharp, zinging pain shoots through my skull. Which is what always happens when I try to overcome my amnesia.

After the pain subsides, the reality of my condition causes a dull ache to emerge in my chest. A deep tiredness that creeps out like an animal, climbs onto my shoulders, and keeps me pinned to my bed.

Lara comes over. Hops onto my bedside table. "Dude . . . You took so long in the bathroom that I had to end up using the *litter box.* I hope you're happy with yourself—because you're cleaning it."

I don't reply.

"*Oh.*" Lara notices the photo and purses her lips. "Jasper? You okay?"

"Fine. Just living my best life, as always," I reply.

Is Shadow Girl also living her best life? Or did she . . .

Lara reaches out to paw at my shoulder and smiles. "Hey, I know what will cheer you up: a rerun of *Friends.*"

"I don't feel like it."

"Really?"

Lara starts singing the *Friends* theme song. Her voice is shrill, and I know from experience that the only way to get Lara to hush is to turn on the TV.

We slump on the sofa, and I flick the channel over to *Friends.*

Tonight's episode shows a flashback of the characters when they were in college, but I can't enjoy it. What were my plans for *my* life? In my bedroom, right next to that Ewok village diorama, is a dog-eared pile of college brochures. What did I want to be? Was I going to college? Did I have big dreams? Honestly, I have no fucking clue.

The show's laugh track seems to mock me.

"Why do we even watch this shit?" I ask Lara.

The cat shrugs. "I dunno. It's just fun watching people hanging out and, like, living their lives and doing shit." She gives me a look that says, *Unlike us*.

That night I dream about stumbling upon Central Perk. I gaze through the window of the *Friends* café. Rachel, Joey, Chandler, Ross, and Monica are seated on their orange couch, watching Phoebe strum her guitar. On the back wall, in the space that once held the menu, is a hell portal about six feet tall. The portal is guarded by a Vanguard soldier. None of the café patrons seem overly concerned. Everyone is just going about their lives. Part of me wants to enter the café and hang with the *Friends* gang, but what would I say to them? Even in dreams, I have no damn backstory.

Then . . .

A flicker of light catches my eye. Four ghostly silhouettes—wriggling humanoid wraiths that no one else seems to notice—gather around the portal to touch it. I seize up as the portal turns bright neon red.

The wraiths step aside, and with a rumble, the portal expands to twice its size and gushes a tide of dark matter.

No . . . not dark matter, but *monsters*. Hundreds of tendrils, claws, and slimy gruesome bodies. People scream. The dark mass swells up to swallow the Vanguard soldier, then the couch with Ross, Rachel, Monica, Chandler, and Joey on it. They barely get out the start of a scream before they've been eaten. Phoebe tries to use her guitar to beat back the monsters, but an octopus tentacle lashes out and snares her.

Before I can run away, the tide of monsters smashes through the café windows. A demon claw grabs at my pant leg, pulling me to the ground. I scream as I try to kick my way free.

Abruptly the tide freezes.

I cannot get untangled from the mass, but I gaze up to see the four wraiths standing in front of me, their bodies twisting and shifting, as though they cannot decide how long their limbs should be. I can't see their faces as they study me. But . . . maybe they don't have faces.

"Please . . . no!" I stammer.

Wordlessly, they step aside, and hundreds of demons pile on top of me, burying me alive, silencing my screams with their bodies.

I wake startled, sweating. My bedsheets are glued to my body, and my pulse is hammering. Over the last few months, I've had countless nightmares where wraiths transform a portal and cause it to gush demons. All the dreams have seemed ultra-HD realistic. Some have even felt *real*, in the moment.

I wander to the doorway of my parents' bedroom. "Hey,

Mom. Dad," I whisper to their nonexistent ghosts. "I had another . . . nightmare."

I try to imagine what my folks would've told me, but I can't even remember their voices. These days there's only one person who'll ever tell me things will be okay. "Chill, Jasper," I mumble as I crouch in the shadows. "That was just a nightmare. There's nothing to be afraid of."

If only I sounded more convincing.

4

Retail Blues, Blood Reds

The next morning, I awake to the sound of the TV. Bleary-eyed, I wander into the living room to see Lara watching Vanguard's streaming channel. Specifically, a city update from Lieutenant Davey Shiner—a hero of Hell Portal Day. Shiner looks like he was lifted from a Hollywood action movie, and Lara has a *huge* crush on him.

Lieutenant Shiner is talking about a recent battle on Gazer Boulevard—a derelict neighborhood occupied by homeless people. Recently, demons streamed out of a portal in Gazer, and the segment shows a picture of this giant M&M with *teeth*. Vanguard put it down easily (chocolate melts, after all) and saved the day with no casualties.

"We at Vanguard are committed to protecting everyone, no matter where you come from or who you are," says Shiner.

Lara notices me and waves a cute paw before calling out, "Breakfast?"

"Morning to you too."

I grab us bowls of strawberry ice cream—our daily breakfast since last week when we ran out of cereal—and I sit beside her on the couch. I should get actual breakfast, but secretly I like pretending I'm on a hidden-camera show called *Adulting Fails*. Maybe one day, my folks will spring out to yell, "That's it, kiddo! Not *another* spoonful!" before letting me know, "*Surprise! We're alive!*"

Lara stops eating to stare at me. "Dude, you know you look like shit?"

"Same dream," I mutter.

"*Again?* Maybe it's time to think about moving?" She places a paw on my arm. "It can't be easy living in—"

"I'm fine. I'm not moving anywhere," I tell her. "It was just a nightmare."

Before she can say anything else, I walk to a window and stare down at a dumpster in the alley below. "Hey. Do you think it's possible I used to have a girlfriend?"

Lara sputters on her ice cream. "Uh, um . . . *surrrre.*"

I try not to read into that. "The shadow girl in *that* photo . . . I can't help but think there's more about her in my mind somewhere."

Lara pushes away her ice cream and sighs. "Sorry, Romeo. Wish I could help unlock your amnesia, but sadly I don't have that power."

I frown. "You mean some demons have mental powers?"

Her ears prick up. "Uh, no."

Before I can dwell on that, my phone timer goes off.

"Bah, I need to get ready for work."

Minutes later, I'm out on the street.

It took a while after my accident for me to be able to stand without puking. But once I could and I finally got up the courage to go outside, it was like stepping into a photo of a city I'd read about but never been to. I knew so much about Sundown City—street names, bus lines, too many details around the scandal involving a mayor's dick pics—but nothing felt familiar. Nothing felt lived in, nothing triggered any memories.

That hasn't changed since. Today's no different. Walking through my hometown, I might as well be exploring the Ewok village.

I head toward the mart while schoolkids skip down the sidewalk, clouds shimmer, and everywhere I look, dozens of new pastel-green Vanguard Corporation roadblocks have turned up.

I don't know whether there's a nearby threat, or if VC is upgrading security, but either way, my normal route to the Here For You mart is blocked. I have to use the Vanguard app to get directions to my destination. It takes me on a meandering route, but at least I get a VC point for every roadblock I pass. Everyone is doing the same; the air is filled with the sounds of coins clinking.

I spot a church with open doors. Glimpse a full morning service.

"Names have power," a pastor calls out to everyone.

"Vanguard can call the demons 'extra-dimensional creatures' and the world beyond the portals the 'hostile other dimension.' But everyone knows that those infernal creatures are *demons* . . . and the 'HOD' is nothing other than Satan's dominion. My friends . . . it is *hell!*"

Is it though? I wonder.

The portals are apparently *one-way* openings. Even VC hasn't been able to send anything into the HOD—no cameras, no soldiers.

"We must *always* speak truth," says the pastor, holding his hands out to his congregation. "To truly fight evil, we must always denounce the darkness for exactly what it is!"

My Vanguard app sends me a notification: **VANGUARD x SUBWAY®! Get a free Soldier Sub if you redeem this coupon within 15 mins!**

All around me, phones chime in unison, probably with the very same coupon. Without thinking too much about it, I follow the crowd to the nearest Subway. I've got just enough time.

A dozen steps in, a distant shout draws my attention.

I halt to stare at a barbwire fence covered in STAY CLEAR signs. Vanguard has placed a metal meshing behind the barbwire, which grays out the enclosed area beyond. I move closer anyway and can just barely make out a concrete building with barred windows. Guards are stationed along the perimeter.

The shouting is coming from inside that structure, the local Vanguard asylum. It's the home of the "Doomies":

folks who lost their minds in the wake of Hell Portal Day. They've developed a condition called Doomsday Delirium. Their apocalyptic hallucinations make it impossible for them to function. Every time I pass here, my stomach sinks. What causes Doomsday Delirium? Could *I* catch it? Is my amnesia the first sign?

I attempt to get a closer look, opening my phone camera to try to use the zoom. But my camera app shows a pixelated screen, and the Vanguard app instantly sends me a message: **Restricted Area. Stay Clear.**

I'm about to walk away, but I spot a dark-haired guy who must be about my age peering at me through the barbwire fence. He's gotten close enough to the fencing to poke at the mesh, and it distorts briefly, as though I'm facing my reflection in a circus mirror.

"People say we're crazy . . . but so are *you*."

I flinch. "I . . . I'm not—"

"Crazy? Yes, you are. You, with your constant *ding, ding, dings!*" The stranger pretends to wield a smartphone and mimics notification chimes. He gestures at the people on the sidewalk, who are walking with eyes glued to phones, all chasing different VC prizes, points, freebies. The Doomie folds his arms. "Look around. Look around! Look—"

But then the guy staggers backward and starts convulsing. Before I can call for help, two female doctors dart over. They check his vitals and talk to him in calm tones as they lead him back toward the asylum.

"Hey," a Vanguard patrolman calls out, stalking over to my patch of the sidewalk. He's got a rifle strapped across his chest and gestures for me to scram. "Keep it moving, kiddo."

I'm about to leave, but then he eyes my work vest and gives me a nod of respect. As though me being a Hell Zone worker makes me a minor league hero, or the next, next, *next* best thing to one.

"You work in *that* Here For You mart?" he asks.

"That's right—"

"Great! Can you do me a favor and hide some of those super cheap yogurt cups with the gorilla logo? They *always* run out before I get there."

My shoulders slump a little. "Oh. Sorry, man. Discount's over," I tell him, and then just continue on my way.

After my accident, I spent days exploring the city, hoping I'd stumble upon the burning dumpster, fantasizing that Shadow Girl would be standing there amid the swirling ash, ready to tell me with a smile, "Finally! I've been waiting for you!" But instead, days in, I came upon a dimly lit neon sign that read, HERE FOR YO (the *U* had burned out), and I recognized it as the logo on a work vest in my closet.

Underneath the sign was a free-standing building with moldy walls and grimy windows. I stepped into the store, and while nothing looked familiar, the clerks who saw me did a double take.

"There you are!" a voice boomed, and I turned to see a

bald guy in a blue shirt. His name pin was ridiculously tiny on his enormous chest: *GULLY GORMAN. MANAGER.* "About fucking time! We thought you died."

I blinked. "Um . . . So, I . . . work here?"

Gully frowned. "*What?*"

I gestured at the giant bandage on my forehead. "My head. I just . . . things are . . . fuzzy. I don't really *remember* stuff."

Gully stepped closer as if he wanted to stare straight *into me*, like he was trying to x-ray my damn brain, then abruptly stepped backward. "You . . . don't remember?"

I took in my reflection in the mirror panel of a sunglass stand. "I mean, I know some stuff, like, you know, end caps and 'stock rotation.' That's a thing, right?" I said, pointing at a display at the end of an aisle.

Gully looked as though he wanted to jam a pencil between his eyes—or mine. "Ah, for fuck's sake! *Seriously?*" he muttered.

I started to retreat from his human Rottweiler vibe.

"Where are you going?" Before I could reply to that, Gully grabbed my shoulders. "You're hopeless . . . but you're not going to leave us one person short right now."

And that is how I came to work at the Here For You mart—again.

My morning shift begins, but the mart hasn't yet opened. And I find myself lingering near the entrance. The AC makes a growl-like sputter, and I shiver as I notice claw marks on the floor from yesterday's fun. Which makes me wonder, as always, *Why the fuck am I still here?*

My feet crunch on something: the photo booth strip with four pictures of Kyle Kuan. I pick it up and study the images. In that last photo square, Kyle is staring right at the camera, right at me.

Voices echo from the distant back room, and I realize I'm late for the morning staff meeting. I pocket the photo strip and head for the break room. By the time I get there, my twelve fellow clerks are already seated.

Most of them are around my age. Thanks to Vanguard's Freedom-16 Act, it's legal for teens sixteen and older to do hell-related jobs. We're adults when we're asked to mop blood, but conveniently teens when it comes to payroll.

Gully shoots me a glare that says, *You're late again.*

"Sorry," I mumble.

I spot a seat at the back. It's behind our "veteran" F-16s: Dean, Penelope, and Norm. They've been here the longest and treat the job like it's some kind of inside joke. The guys both have patchy beards. They've probably only just started shaving. Penelope has a neck tattoo, which looks maybe self-done and still red and painful. When I nod hello and try to shuffle by them to a seat, they stretch their legs to block my path. Whatever. I'll sit up front with the newest F-16 hires, who probably won't be here next week anyway.

Gully gestures for me to hurry up.

"Sorry," I repeat.

"Timing is everything," Gully calls out, punctuating each word while still glaring at me. "Listen up, turds. In retail, timing really *is* everything. It underpins each shift, rotation, and sale. And now that we're headed for the end of November, timing is gonna be more crucial than ever. After all . . . what event are we heading toward, people?"

"Black Friday," we chorus, most of us groaning—except for our resident weirdos, Robbie and Jono, who seem to *enjoy* working here. They both sound legit excited.

Gully claps his hands together. "Yes! Black Friday is only four days away, and I recently received a *very* interesting email from head office. It seems they've decided to challenge each Here For You mart to a 'Black Friday Bonus Bonanza.' The store that draws the biggest profit will receive a *mega bonus*—a cash pool that the winning store's manager can split with their team."

My peers stare at one another, blinking. The only "splits" we ever get here are diabolical morning-afternoon split shifts.

"A shared *cash bonus*?" Robbie asks carefully.

Gully nods. "To share between me, the manager, and you, the staff."

Translation: Gully will probably split it 90/10.

Robbie beams, and I sigh. This is going to be more disappointing for Robbie than the time he tried to use the break room microwave to make "hot-air balloons."

"To get this bonus, we'll need to bring in the most profit of any Here For You mart in the country. Ergo, this place will need to be a shopper's paradise." Gully rubs his hands together. "Head office suggests that we treat this like a game. And, as you all know, all games have winners . . . and winners get rewards!"

Gully starts doling out instructions for Black Friday prep, and my attention drifts to a TV playing quietly in a corner. A morning-show host is interviewing Lieutenant Shiner about the rumors that he's going to be the next star of *The Bachelor*. Shiner laughs good-naturedly but then pivots to a more important topic: VC's plans for Black Friday:

"Unlike last year, Vanguard will not be instituting crowd limits on shopping zones. Instead, we'll be amping up security and allowing all approved retail venues to partake in this fantastic event!"

By *all approved retail venues*, he means Relatively Safe Hell Zone stores are allowed to join the madness. Because hey, retail is the multibillion-dollar baby that must be protected at all costs.

Gully drones on about Black Friday's big-ticket items. And my attention drifts again to Kyle Kuan, who pushes through the break room door and crashes our meeting without seeming to give a damn. As a trainee Vanguardian, Kyle spends her shifts patrolling the "safe" parts of the store. (Unless the mart's two other guards are both incapacitated, she isn't allowed inside aisle nine.)

Seeing her, I think of a recent memory from about a month ago. I was standing in the toy aisle when I noticed a dark shape peeking over the aisle's top shelf. At first, I worried it was some kind of weird gray-brown monster, but then I realized it was actually just the soles of Kyle's boots. Kyle was lying on the top shelf, staring above her. She'd gotten her hands on a toy gun and was shooting suction darts at the ceiling. No one seemed to notice her but me.

Without asking, I got a stepladder and climbed up to the top of the next aisle. I lay down parallel to her.

I turned and saw Kyle's face in profile. *Shit. What am I doing?* I was about to climb down, my heart racing, but then Kyle turned and frowned at me. And I couldn't help but wonder if I'd done something to annoy her. *Fuck it.*

"Hey," I whispered.

I pulled out my scanner gun and pretended to use it as a firearm, shooting off laser beams into distant mannequin heads. I blew the smoke off the imaginary barrel, and our eyes met again, and Kyle seemed to look right *through* me. Sighing silently, I fired another laser beam at nothing in particular.

My beam hit a ceiling-mounted security mirror, and the light reflected into my right eye.

"*Gargh! Shit!*" I hissed.

Kyle let out a chuckle, a hint of a smile even tugged at her lips, and suddenly I was *exactly* where I wanted to be.

I felt like we were both trapped in an identical Venn diagram. One with three labeled circles—*Why did I get up this morning?*; *What am I doing?*; *When is this all going to make sense?*—that overlapped in the middle to form a section labeled *YOUR LIFE*.

Somehow, I felt like she was someone who truly . . . *got it*.

But before I could say anything, Kyle lowered her gaze, yellow bangs falling over her eyes, her shoulders tensed up, and in one acrobatic move, she hopped to the ground like she wanted to get away from me as fast as she could.

"Jasper!" Gully yells.

Kyle is gone, and Gully is standing over me. I'm about to apologize for spacing out, but he clears his throat and adds, "All games have winners . . . and *losers*. With that in mind, anyone who does not pull their weight in the lead-up to Black Friday is a loser and will be fired."

I grip the sharp edges of the photo booth strip of Kyle that's in my pocket.

"I *swear* I won't let you down, Gully," I promise, before realizing I've done the one thing no retail worker should ever do. I've admitted to my boss that I *need* this job.

Gully looks me over, sneers, then wanders outside. He returns with a sandwich board that has a game wheel stuck to it. It's the knockoff *Wheel of Fortune* wheel that we used in the store for some earlier promotion. Dean and Norm snicker.

Gully grabs a Sharpie, scratches out the number values on the wheel, and, in their place, scribbles down chores. "Step over here, Jasper. These are all Black Friday prep items. Give it a spin and you'll do whatever you land on."

I walk over to the wheel.

The shape has labels such as *BF toilet cleaning* and *BF mascot duty*. I don't know what to aim for, but seeing no other option, I suck in a breath and spin the wheel.

The arrow part lands on the words *floor prep.*

That doesn't sound so bad, does it?

Turns out, "floor prep" means adding metallic sticker dots to the floor to create a silver path through the aisles. Because Gully wants to have "a path like on a board game." To do this, I'm on my hands and knees with a roll of thousands of stickers.

Such bullshit.

A dozen feet away, a woman is carrying a little boy, and she points me out to him, as though I'm a duck in a pond. "See *him*?" she whispers to her kid. "Dream big, sweetie! Or that could be you one day!"

Apparently we're playing the board game Life. The Retail Worker Edition!

I turn my back to the shoppers, only to see Penelope and Dean heading my way, laughing. There it is again—that vibe they give off that working here is an inside joke. But what's the joke? That if life's going to eff you over, you might as well be an F-16 and get the hazard pay?

They spot me. Penelope raises a brow, as though I'm some sort of mental hospital escapee. Before I know it, she takes out a tiny vintage Polaroid camera and snaps a picture.

"Do you *mind*?" I bark, but she and Dean walk off, probably to put my picture on the Employee of the Month board.

Awesome. . . .

I realize I accidentally pushed my sticker roll under the aisle edge beside me. I reach in to grab it—but end up extracting a pair of grimy dentures.

"Fuck!" I hiss.

But when I catch my breath, I sigh and turn the dentures into a talking hand puppet: "Lighten up, buddy. . . . Working in a discount mart isn't all bad. This job comes with free *dental* solutions!"

Footsteps emerge.

A young Vanguard soldier is staring at me. He takes off his helmet and frowns. I chuck aside the dentures. "I'm kidding. We *don't* have a dental plan here," I mutter.

"Jasper?" he asks.

I stand up and mirror his frown.

"*Hah!* It *is* you!" His brown cheeks crease into a smile. He fist-bumps me on my shoulder and causes me to sway back. "How are you?"

"Uh . . . good?" I reply.

His armored jacket has an embroidered tag: *C. GUTIERREZ*. He sees me staring at his uniform and says, "Yep! I now work for the Vanguard Corporation. Crazy, right? I'm here to replace one of the guards in aisle nine." He steps back to take in my uniform. "So, you work in this place, huh?"

I'm choosing to ignore the faint wincing sound.

"How long has it been since we saw each other?" he asks.

"A long time . . . ?"

"Since our early graduation, right?"

So we're school friends? "We graduated early?"

I'd always assumed I dropped out of school.

"Yeah, dude. And I'm still bummed about it," says Gutierrez. "I thought that once Vanguard repaired the city, we'd leave the lockdowns and get to finish sophomore year. Never thought they'd deem our school too hard to repair—and just graduate our entire class."

"We never got the chance to do junior and senior year?"

"Nah, man. But I guess Vanguard needed new bodies in the workforce, what with all the deaths from Hell Portal Day." Gutierrez narrows his eyes. "Ugh, why am I telling you what you already know? You were there. *Duh.*"

Finally, someone who has answers about my past.

"Yeah, I know I should know about this graduation stuff. It's just—"

Gutierrez sighs and says, "Man! I haven't thought about that graduation for so long. I'd almost forgotten how pissed I was."

"What do you mean?" I ask.

Gutierrez leans against a shelf and stares into the distance. "Well, I didn't lose anyone to demons—and I'm super *grateful*—but damn, I was supposed to finish school. Become a doctor. Maybe move overseas. I just assumed my life would change into something bigger, but instead . . . we get *shortchanged* into graduating in a Wendy's parking lot on a random Wednesday morning."

"I feel you," I reply, not knowing quite what else to say.

Gutierrez straightens up and says, "Do you remember the speech that that Vanguard recruiter gave us?"

Before I can say anything, Gutierrez imitates a gruff voice:

"'Listen up, kids! What more can school teach you? You know as much about survival in a broken world as any adult. You know shit all.'" Gutierrez mimics a mic drop, then cocks a brow. "You okay, dude?"

I brush back my hair to touch my forehead scar, muttering, "I don't actually remember *ever* being okay."

I finally tell him all about my head trauma.

When I'm finished, his eyes are saucer wide. "*Amnesia? You sayin' you can't remember anything?*"

"Nada." I shrug. "What do you remember about me?"

Gutierrez scratches at his patchy facial hair. "I dunno. I remember you were in a lot of my classes—algebra, biology— but mostly you just . . . kept to yourself. You were kinda quiet, but not creepy quiet. Shy. I don't know that we ever had, like, an actual conversation before today."

I'm unable to stifle a huge sigh. "That's . . . all?"

I've scanned UPC barcodes to reveal longer descriptions.

Gutierrez lowers his gaze and scuffs at the ground. "Well . . . I *do* remember one more thing: during our graduation, you were so motionless, just staring into the distance, like you were barely breathing." He pauses. "You lost people on Hell Portal Day, didn't you?"

That graduation was probably a few months after that tragic Christmas.

"My parents," I whisper.

Gutierrez shakes his head. "Geez. I'm so sorry."

I'm not sure what to say. Neither is he.

Kyle Kuan walks past the aisle, and Gutierrez cranes his neck in her direction. "Hah! I was right earlier. That *is* Kyle Kuan."

I blink. "You . . . know her too?"

Now it's Gutierrez who seems bewildered. "Yeah, Kyle K. was in our grade." He tips his head to the side. "Don't you guys, like, talk here? I think I remember once seeing you guys hanging out in the cafeteria. Weren't you friends?"

"*Seriously?*" The word *friends* repeats over and over in my head, rolling into a distorted roar, before someone calls out my name.

In the distance, Gully barks at me to get back to work.

"We can talk later, dude," says Gutierrez before he wanders off.

I can barely focus on where I'm sticking down metallic dots. My attention is spiraling around what I've learned—about my graduation, about *Kyle*—and I find myself trying to imagine these things. My attempt to hot-wire my brain into showing me some *actual* memories.

But no matter how hard I try, all I get is the familiar zinging pain in my skull. When I finally give up, a dull ache swirls around inside me.

Will things ever change?

I begin to feel so fatigued that I force myself not to *think* for a little while. I try to focus on work. I lay down sticker dot after dot and attempt to lose myself in the repetition. Time passes. A random shopper tousles my hair. Another uses my back as a place for her coffee cup. I feel I've been at it for miles, but when I check my progress . . .

I've barely stickered two yards.

A *click* draws my attention. I turn to see a nearby TV flicker with a red ⊠—the symbol for a local group of hackers known as Suckerpunch—and suddenly the screen shows the bright red words *VANGUARD LIES!*

Still trying to distract myself from *myself*, I wander over to view this latest cable hack from Suckerpunch. It's a message about the recent demon attack in Gazer Boulevard, where the M&M monsters were rampaging. The hackers show a clip of VC soldiers waiting on the sidelines. They allege that VC let the battle spill out of control in order to clear away homeless folks—and allow them to redevelop the area.

Could it be true? Honestly, I don't know.

Abruptly, the cable hack shows a bunch of bloodstained sidewalks from the battle. A female shopper halts in front of the TV and holds out her arms, as though she wants to embrace the bloody images. Oh, wait— She's trying to measure the screen without using a tape measure.

"Humph. Nah," she mumbles, wandering off.

Only then does the cable hack finally get shut down.

"And we now return to our regularly scheduled pro-gramming, folks," I whisper, only to turn around and freeze—

As Kyle walks past.

Vanguard soldiers always wear multiple Kevlar pieces: shin guards, chest protectors, helmets, arm braces. But as a trainee, Kyle only has a Kevlar vest. She's paired it with a black tee, cutoff shorts, shiny oil-slick tights, and combat boots. Her helmet and flamethrower hang off her back thanks to a cross-body strap.

Kyle passes a shelf and grabs a few highlighter pens before stalking over to the sunglasses rack. She eyes her neon-yellow hair in a mirror panel and finds a section where the color has faded to reveal bleached strands. She uses a yellow high-lighter to "dye" the blank section of hair.

In the distance, the portal has started humming eerily. But Kyle keeps staring into the tiny strip of mirror. A shop-per rotates the rack, mirrors carousel-ing, but Kyle doesn't react.

The rack spins back to its earlier position, which is when Kyle spots me via the mirror.

"Yeah?" she asks, eyes sharp.

How do I even talk to her? Whenever I interact with

Kyle, I spin a *Wheel of Fortune* wheel with only three labels: *AGGRAVATED, BORED, INDIFFERENT.* It's pointless, and yet . . . I'm *always* ready to give the wheel a spin.

"Uh, thanks for the save yesterday," I tell her.

"Sure," she replies mutedly.

She's settled on *INDIFFERENT,* but I don't give up as I ask, "So . . . do you ever think about high school?"

Unblinking, Kyle shrugs and says, "Not really."

"Oh," I reply.

Kyle walks away, and I think Gutierrez must be wrong. How could Kyle and I have ever been friends in school? Or even casual acquaintances? But then Kyle halts a dozen steps ahead and turns slightly, as though ready to look back at me, only to pause.

Wait. Does she remember me?

But then she seems to think better of continuing our conversation and heads off again. I want to chase after her, but I sense she won't say more. So instead, I take in a deep breath and try to get my brain to show me a memory of Kyle. But just like before, my attempt to find a lost memory causes my head to zing. I try to push through the pain, but the zinging sensation explodes behind my eyes . . . and then cuts out into darkness.

Someone calls out my name. I'm staring at the ceiling, and halogen lights cut into my vision. Blinking, I look around to find myself sprawled atop what was once a pyramid of stacked toilet paper.

Gutierrez is poking my shoulder. "Jasper! Wake up, dude."

I rub at my temples. "What . . . happened?"

Gutierrez helps me sit up and then tells me I collapsed onto the toilet paper pyramid. "Um, you need me to call the VC medic?"

I take in a steadying breath. "No, I just . . . think I finally pushed it too hard."

"Pushed what?"

I take a deep breath. No use in holding back when I've already told him so much. "It's my amnesia. Whenever I try to find a memory, it's like my brain rebels. This time it went full guerrilla warfare." My upper lip is damp, and I realize I've got a nosebleed. I try to wipe away blood. "*Shit*. . . . Just when I thought things couldn't get weirder."

Gutierrez frowns. "Jasper, dude, what's going on with you?"

I shrug. "I don't even know where to start. I have super vivid apocalyptic nightmares about the portals. Each dream shows chaos, and I wake up with the sense that they're, like, pulling from some sort of real future danger."

Gutierrez stiffens, so I quickly add, "But they're just dreams."

He studies me, then helps me get up and leads me to the garden section in the back of the store. Standing beside a plastic fern, he looks around to check we're alone. "Dude, I don't know how else to say this, but it sounds like you might be developing the Doomsday Delirium."

"Hah!" I chuckle. "You think I'm becoming a Doomie? Seriously?"

When he doesn't move a muscle, my laughter becomes strangled.

"Don't joke about that shit, dude."

Gutierrez lowers his voice to add, "Look, I don't think amnesia is a symptom—but vivid apocalypse nightmares *and* trouble with everyday functioning? Those are definitely initial symptoms of Doomsday Delirium. You should—"

"I don't have trouble functioning."

He raises a brow. "You *just* face-planted into a small hill of toilet paper."

"C'mon, that's just a side effect of my head trauma," I interrupt.

"What if this has *nothing* to do with your accident?" Gutierrez rolls his shoulders, wavers. "Look, I'm not a doctor, but if you *are* going through Doomsday Delirium, you *need* to get medical attention before it spirals into full-blown psychosis. You need to visit a VC med facility, get checked out."

I flinch. "I don't need some asylum prison—"

Gutierrez folds his arms. "Is that what you think VC does to Doomies? Imprisons them? Jasper, they're spending millions helping whatever Doomies they find."

My thoughts go to what I've seen around the local asylum. I want to argue about the barbwire and camera-censorship field, but then I remember how that young guy had a seizure.

"Has anyone ever recovered?" I ask.

Gutierrez looks away briefly. "From what I know, VC tries to get Doomies to face the hell-related trauma that caused their Doomsday Delirium—in order to get them to heal. It's a whole thing."

"Face my trauma? Like, you mean, both my parents dying on Hell Portal Day?"

Gutierrez hesitates but shakes his head. "Nah, dude. If you are starting to develop DD, then the catalyst event has to be more recent than Hell Portal Day. Like, I dunno . . . maybe something that occurred a few months ago?"

I'm not sure what to say.

"But I don't remember a catalyst within the last few months—and I don't remember anything from before that—"

I'm interrupted when the lights flicker with a crackle.

Gutierrez spins away, turns his attention toward aisle nine. He signals for me to follow and leads the way as we creep closer. We're barely a dozen steps away when the lighting returns to normal. Peering into the quarantine zone, I spot Ollie Sheffield standing guard, alone, opposite the portal. His helmet and armor cover most of him, save for his pale fingers and the lower part of his face.

The air is filled with a dry electricity. I can almost taste the static.

Gutierrez starts unlocking the gate, and I call out, "Hey, Ollie. Everything okay?"

No response.

"Ollie?"

As usual, Ollie doesn't bother to acknowledge anyone who isn't VC. Then again, he practices that all-important workplace rule: *You focus on your shit, and I'll focus on mine.* Something I should be grateful for, considering that he's saved my life on at least two occasions.

Gutierrez enters the quarantine and talks quietly with Ollie.

I know I should leave them be, but my heart skips a beat when the in-aisle lighting flickers again. Seconds later, Gutierrez tells me to step back for safety.

A bunch of skateboarding teens roll toward aisle nine. "Yo! *Please*," I tell them, gesturing for them to get off the boards. They snort but do as I ask in order to get close to aisle nine and gawk.

I'm about to shoo them off, but then the portal hisses and an object comes fluttering out. A black envelope with a white postage stamp. Is Satan looking for a pen pal?

"Great. Junk mail," Gutierrez cracks.

The skater teens are staring at the envelope, rapt.

So am I.

"Whatever," says Ollie. He uses a flamethrower burst to destroy the letter, then peers over at the teen shoppers. "Show's over, kiddies. Scram."

The teenagers sigh but head away.

I'm also about to wander off, until I notice that the portal is still quivering.

I clear my throat. "Um, guys . . ."

The hole's quiver turns quickly to a rumble, and then a

humanoid thing jumps out. It's six feet tall and covered from head to toe in what look like scales—but are actually, *holy shit*, postage stamps. The creature has no eyes, but it opens a jagged maw and howls.

My feet are rooted in place.

Ollie and Gutierrez use their flamethrowers to bathe the monster in fire. They turn the postage stamps to ash, then scorch the underlying humanoid. The air fills with a stench of burning paper and roasted flesh. The monster shrieks. Fire chars it into a silhouette.

It slumps to the ground and goes silent.

All around me, shoppers are staring in aisle nine's direction, wide-eyed and stiff with fear. Then, a moment later, when it seems the worst has passed, everyone sighs and resumes whatever they were doing. Everyone except for the skater teens. They hiss at me as I shoo them away again, but they don't fight me and instead wander off farther into the store.

In aisle nine, Gutierrez douses the demon with a second blast of fire, even though it is completely motionless. The air fills with smoke.

"Enough," says Ollie. "We don't want to set off the store's smoke detectors."

Gutierrez breaks from his fire-throwing trance and shuts it down.

Ollie pushes up his helmet visor and says, "Good. It's dead. Now let's dispose of this fucker."

He grabs a Vanguard-issue chainsaw. A super powerful but highly unwieldy tool that the guards use when they shift from monster slaying to monster cleanup. He lifts it and says, "But first, *head check*."

Head check. He means lop off the head just in case.

Ollie tightens his grip on the chainsaw's pull cord, but before he can yank it on, the monster springs to its feet. It grabs Ollie's and Gutierrez's necks, slams their helmets together, then chortles as they fall to the ground.

Ollie rises, woozily, as the monster roars. He tries to grab the fallen chainsaw, but the creature punches him in the chest—and knocks him clear across the aisle.

"Ollie!" I shout, but he's not responding, not moving.

Gutierrez staggers to his feet. His helmet has fallen off. He grabs the chainsaw and jerks the cord so it roars to life. He slams it into the monster's back, cutting a deep, bloody gash. But almost instantly the chainsaw jams and conks out, lodged in the monster. The creature spins around, flexing its back to dislodge the chainsaw.

The monster lunges at Gutierrez, but he's quick on his feet, evades the blows, and unsheathes a sword strapped to his back. Gutierrez swings the sword, hard. The demon blocks the move with a forearm but ends up getting that limb cleaved off just above the elbow.

The creature howls and collapses to the floor in pain.

Gutierrez twirls his sword in a figure eight. "Look at me," he calls out to it. "Yeah. I'm talking to you, you little shit. Look at me! You sent us a postcard? Well, here's a message for you—*We are not afraid*." He kicks the monster, mutters "Fuck it," and then lifts his sword high like it's time to end the beast.

But before Gutierrez can bring the blade down, the monster opens its mouth as wide as it can, and postage stamps come flying out. Not just a few, but hundreds, maybe thousands. They're pouring out of it fast and furious like a tornado in a post office. The paper whacks into Gutierrez with enough force to knock him clear onto his ass. While he's down, the monster reaches into its chest and pulls out a huge black stamp. It licks the back and then plasters the stamp over Gutierrez's face.

Gutierrez starts to panic and thrash. He can't breathe. He's clawing at the stamp but can't get it off. Meanwhile the monster lifts a fist—

"Hey! You there!"

Ollie. He's back on his feet at the far end of the aisle.

The creature scurries toward him, and my attention shoots back to Gutierrez. I have to do something. I look at the gate and try to recall the keypad code for the lock. I think I once saw Ollie enter the numbers 0219, so I try it and the gate opens.

Suddenly I stand rigid in the threshold of aisle nine.

Move! Come on! Do something!

Kyle rushes past me and darts over to Gutierrez's side. She opens a water bottle, pours it on his face to soften the stamp. She pulls at the paper's lower edge, but the paper keeps tearing. She's going too slow. . . .

Shuddering, I force myself over to Kyle's side. Instead of trying to rip the paper all the way to Gutierrez's upper lip, I jam my fingers in approximately where I think his mouth would be. The stamp rips, and he nearly gags on my hand, but then he sucks in a breath. He's got air again.

The monster has backed Ollie into a corner, but the guard is using his flamethrower to keep it back and melt it down. But somehow, the demon keeps pushing on through the flames. Soon, it's so close that Ollie has no choice but to chuck aside his flamethrower and use his own sword to fight back.

Kyle helps Gutierrez remove most of the stamp on his eyes. He seems dazed, but Kyle helps him to his feet and hands him his sword.

A yell fills the air. The monster has knocked aside Ollie's weapon. The creature has gripped Ollie by the neck and lifted him up. The monster bites his left arm, and I hear a sound that makes me think of splintering wood and ripping fabric. Ollie screams. The monster releases him, turns around, and I see a huge tongue sticking out of its mouth—no, wait, not a tongue, but an *arm*! Ollie's arm.

Gutierrez charges at the beast, sword up, yelling. The blade sinks into the creature's neck, lodged. *"Time to return . . . to sender!"* Gutierrez swears as he lops the beast's head off.

The creature instantly crumbles to ash.

Gutierrez runs over to Ollie, then pulls out his belt to create a tourniquet to keep Ollie from bleeding out. Kyle uses her walkie to call Vanguard HQ for an emergency evac.

But me? I can barely stay on my feet. Nothing seems real. Not the monster we saw, not Ollie's blood all over the floor.

"Dear God . . . ," I whisper.

I hear footsteps, then turn to see a boy—maybe ten or eleven, in a green hoodie—enter the aisle threshold. He stares wide-eyed at Ollie, then peeks at a phone in his small hands. Abruptly, I hear a chime from his phone.

"*Four hundred VC points!*" the boy breathes.

He bounces a little, and I realize what's happened. The VC app has sensed a monster attack—based on Kyle's call to Vanguard, or maybe the CCTV—and it's awarded the boy points to compensate him for witnessing violence.

"What the fuck is wrong with you!" I roar at the kid.

Finally, my legs do what my brain tells them to, and I chase the kid out into the street, only to see him disappear into the crowd. Fuck, what would I even do if I caught him? What would that change? All around, everything out here looks so *normal*, people casually walking their dogs and picking up shit in little baggies, and I feel that I'm being gaslit by everyone. For weeks I've quested to find a single burning dumpster, but here and now, this *whole city* is a dumpster fire kingdom.

5

Carry On

By the time I'm back in the store, Ollie is outside on a stretcher and being loaded into a Vanguard ambulance. Gully pulls out our WET FLOOR sign, which really ought to read, NOTHING TO SEE HERE, FOLKS!, while Norman mops away at an arrow-shaped streak of blood from aisle nine. And the customers just . . . stare on.

Sighing, Gully proceeds to make a PA announcement: "Attention, shoppers! For a limited time, all Thanksgiving decorations are seventy-five percent off. Hurry over to aisle three and pick up some festive cheer! Offer ends in one hour!"

All the shoppers—including the gawkers near aisle nine and a young woman cowering in a corner—straighten up, look around, and then rush en masse to aisle three to grab the best stuff before it's gone.

A middle-aged woman pokes me in the shoulder. "Aisle three?" she barks.

I can't actually feel my own tongue, or mouth.

"Aisle three? Where is it?"

Before I can point at the giant *3* hanging above an aisle, the woman walks away with a snort. "*Bah.* Someone's got a few screws missing. . . ."

Look, this isn't my first demon attack, or first time seeing the Vanguard ambulance. There was a time when a guard lost a leg and another when a shopper lost an ear. But this is the first time I've gotten such a close-up glimpse of bloodshed—and I feel as though I could pass out or puke or maybe somehow do *both*.

But instead, I do what the other clerks are doing: carry on. We all get back to our Black Friday prep. We fake smiles and dodge shoppers as life drifts by like oh so many dented cans on the sticky conveyor belt of life. We pretend everything is okay.

Except . . . for me this *is* okay. This place accounts for the bulk of my recent memories, which makes it my baseline. This is my normal. This is where everything makes sense—run, hide, scan barcodes, smile when you ought to scream. This is where I actually have something resembling a purpose.

"That's truly fucked," I mumble.

"What's fucked?" says Gary, a thirtysomething clerk with perennially bloodshot eyes, as he arranges the bestselling item in our school section—the lice comb.

"Do you remember a time when something like *today* would've sent you screaming?" I ask.

"You know what they say, man," Gary answers, without looking up. "Not giving a shit is a learned behavior."

Actually, I think it's hopelessness is a learned behavior.

That's what I'm about to say until my gaze takes in the clerks swirling around, and it hits me: Maybe we already know all about those learned behaviors. Maybe this is where we got our damn diplomas.

Gary's wandered off, but I notice a piece of cardboard on the ground where he'd been standing. I crouch to pick it up. It's a postcard with an image of four silhouetted wraiths standing in front of what seems like a portal—just like what I've seen in my dreams.

I drop it, and it lands on its reverse side.

A jagged handwritten scrawl reads: *JASPER. IT'S COMING SOON!*

I stumble backward, and the postcard disintegrates. The whole mart seems to spin as one thought sinks in: It's real! What I've seen in my dreams is real! An actual apocal—

"No, no, no. That's not possible," I hiss, squeezing my eyes shut. *Everything that emerges from portals is inspired by nightmares. You know this. C'mon . . . that postcard is just lifted from your nightmares. That's all.*

Another deep breath.

I throw myself back into something that seems perversely comforting these days: Work. Pointless, shitty work. I continue price-checking but barely make three little *beeps* before a male shopper in ratty pajamas and slippers walks over.

He's holding a toaster, and grunts, "*Replacement.*"

Before I can say anything, he adds that the device keeps burning his bread. Insists that the burning is due to the fact he was sold a "fuckin' expired toaster." (His proof of expiration? The manufacture date printed underneath the unit.) He demands a replacement, and I decide not to try to explain that he probably had the machine on its highest setting.

Instead, I wander off to get him a "fresh" toaster. When I'm back, I lead him to the info desk, get him to sign our replacements form, and then hand him the appliance.

"Hah! That wasn't so hard now, was it?" he asks.

"No, sir," I reply with a tight smile. "Anything else I can do for you?"

"I'd like a refund too."

And. There. It. Is.

Why does everyone think they can have their toast and eat it too?

"Sir, I'm afraid I cannot grant *both* a replacement and a refund."

"Bullshit. I want something for my troubles. I had to take time out of work to come here."

My gaze takes in his pajamas.

I try to explain why it's one or the other—money or toaster—but he says that's unacceptable and demands to see my manager. I'm about to tell him that Gully is unavailable (what *Gully* always insists we say), until he notices my hands and recoils.

"For crying out loud. That's *disgusting*," he huffs.

I finally notice that my hands have flecks of dried blood all over them.

Shit. . . . This is . . . Ollie's blood.

All the voices in the mart disappear, replaced by a remembered echo of Ollie's screams. Now I realize that there are still bloodstains outside the aisle nine gate, and just like that, I'm well and truly outside the city limits of Okayville.

Abruptly, Toaster Guy starts telling me that the blood is unhygienic and that I "have no respect for the people who come here." When I struggle to focus, he shakes his head and says, "Bah! This isn't going anywhere. I need your manager. *Now.*"

I try to get a word in, but he keeps insisting on talking to a manager.

Over and over. And something finally snaps inside me.

After all I've witnessed, *this* is the last thing I can handle. I grab a stapler and slam it on the info counter. "Hey!" I yell four or five times.

And when he finally hushes, I say, "Sir. You were compensated with a replacement."

The man tenses. "I know my rights. This is America. I want my money back—"

"Fine! *Fine!*" I yell as I open my wallet, pull out a twenty, and fling it at the man.

His cheeks redden. "You . . . ! You should be grateful that customers like me come here to—"

"To do what, sir? Compete with monsters to see who's worse?"

His nostrils flare.

The man rolls up his sleeves, as though ready to clock me, but then he takes my twenty bucks, eyes my name tag, and mutters, "I'll be back to speak to your manager."

I should be freaked, but instead, I find the willpower to grab ahold of all my horror and anger and fear and squeeze it into a tiny box inside me. I do the only possible thing right now: offer a fake smile.

"Well, you have a nice day too, sir."

The man leaves with his toaster, and I stumble into the back room to grab some wet wipes from a dispenser. Shaking, I scrub my hands until they're clean, then I take refuge behind the electronics cage. I crouch down, watch my shadow vanish into the dark edges of the room, and wonder, *Did Shadow Girl drown in the darkness?* But instead of dwelling on that—or anything else from today—I quickly try to distract myself.

Most people can lose themselves in memories of happy places. But me? The best I can do is lose myself in trivia from my brain's undamaged general knowledge section. "Animal? Object? Location?" I choose *animal*, randomly pick *turtles* . . .

I think of green sea turtles. How they emerge without parents (relatable, much?) but somehow have this inner programming that tells them *exactly* where to go and how to live their lives. Suddenly I start imagining that I'm a baby sea turtle, wiggling my tiny green ass into an ocean far from all the portals and customers, my body powered by an innate sense of *what to do with my life*. . . .

When I open my eyes, the back room lights are in power-saving mode. Damn. I've somehow fast-forwarded to 7:00 p.m.? The store's closed. Everyone has probably gone home, except for the VC guards, such as Gutierrez, who remain in aisle nine. No one noticed my absence.

I'm about to head for the rear exit, but I hear a rattling from behind some shelves.

And here we go again. . . .

6

The After-Hours Disco

I dart toward a VC wall panel and I'm about to push a red button that reads *EMERGENCY*. Well, until I peer beyond the shelves at a seven-yard-wide square of concrete: the loading area for delivered goods. It's usually a blank space at night, but right now it's *sparkling*.

I spot familiar metallic sticker dots. Someone has strewn hundreds of them on the concrete to create constellations of stars. In the center of it all, an electric fan—the rotating kind—has been covered in more shiny dots and turned into a mirror ball.

Amid the sparkles, Kyle Kuan spins around on a pair of roller skates, her hands, arms, and skates themselves covered in a few more dots, showering diamond lights everywhere. Her yellow hair cascades over her closed eyes. On and on she spins, shimmering, until she skids over the fan's electrical cord.

Kyle stumbles but gets up to stare at her Kevlar vest lying nearby. There's a fresh stain on it—*Ollie's blood*—and she shivers. When she turns away, her eyes line up with me.

Kyle startles.

I call out, "Sorry, I didn't mean to . . ."

Kyle rolls away, and soon, she's sitting in a corner and taking off her skates. I think of leaving her be, but she's taking a long time to undo the skate straps, her eyes focused on the floor. I think she's . . . waiting. Waiting for me—or *anyone*—to go over and ask if she's okay after what we saw up close today.

I move nearer. I try to fix my hair and instantly feel shitty. Ollie was mauled, and all I can think about is trying to impress a girl.

Kyle doesn't react as I sit cross-legged beside her.

"You okay?" I ask quietly.

She doesn't look at me but shrugs, mumbles, "*Yeah.*"

"You sure?"

The silence hangs heavy.

My attention settles on an upside-down heart-shaped scar on the side of her neck. Finally, her head turns slightly toward me, but she cannot bring her gaze higher than my hands clasped in my lap.

"Why did you want to talk about our school?" she asks quietly.

So she *does* remember me from school. Booyah.

Now I'm also staring at my hands. "Dunno. Guess I just want to remember who I was back then. So . . . I could just, maybe, stop feeling like such a *nobody* all the time."

I dare to look up, and I see her finally looking at me.

Would she have known Shadow Girl?

"Uh. So. There was this girl who used to be in my life." At least, I *think* she used to be. "But these days it's like she never existed. Did you remember her?"

Kyle stiffens and gives me a look that seems to say, *What makes you think* I'd *know about that?* And I wonder if we ever shared more than a few words in school. So I pivot and ask, "Whatever. . . . Anyway, how was your shitty day?"

She looks away but takes a while before she mumbles, "Pretty shitty."

My mind blanks, until eventually I admit, "My day was— Well, I found a pair of dentures under an aisle today."

She shrugs. "Gross."

I too roll my shoulders. "Things could always be worse. Last week someone left a Starbucks cup on a shelf. Some dude had peed in it—right up to the *brim*. Some of it spilled onto my shoes."

Kyle cocks a brow. "Are you forgetting last Thursday's penis monster, the one with the acid urine?"

"Oh, I didn't see any of that stuff. I was too busy dealing with a shopper dude who wanted to use *one* discount coupon on a *hundred* rolls of toilet paper—I mean, come on, it's *one coupon per item*, buddy!"

We study each other, then break into soft chuckles. In my head, I can practically hear a laugh track. It's like we're starring in a comedy about Hell Zone workers, where all the violence is only ever PG-13 and the heaviest thing we'll face is some *Will they or won't they?* drama. I can see the title card: *P·O·R·T·A·L·S*.

Kyle clams up. Shit, I've been staring.

"Yeah, our lives are truly *awesome*," she mutters.

"Then why do you always linger around here when you're off duty?" I ask.

"You noticed that?" Kyle asks with a strange, fixed look. She pulls her legs up to her chest, rests her chin on a knee, and her hair curtains over her eyes. I can barely hear her as she mumbles: "This place is fuckin' awful. But . . ." A long pause. "During my shifts, I have no space to think about problems, fears, or *anything*. I'm in the zone, and it's . . . almost like a drug." She looks away and snorts. "I dunno. Whatever. . . ."

But I *do* know what she means. "Does this mean that your after-hours time is the comedown? A crash that you gotta try to ride out?"

Kyle is staring at the sticker dots on her hands, and I realize there's something underneath the bits of silver—flecks of paper, from when she was peeling stamp material off Gutierrez's face. It seems she couldn't remove all the paper, so she covered what remains.

Her expression flattens, as though she's gone far, far beyond the chill comedown and straight into *numbness*. And it terrifies me.

I notice a random collection of roller skates strewn about—Kyle must have tried them all on for size—and I spot one set that could be my fit. I grab them and put them on. All the while, I hope I know how to skate. It feels like I do, like I just need to shake off the cobwebs and wake up some muscle memory.

Kyle raises a brow, but I reach into my pocket for my phone and cue up a song from Lara's "Plushie Partyyyyy!!!" playlist—SG Lewis's "Chemicals." I stick my phone in my pocket, get to my feet as beats stream out, and I quickly realize that gravity works differently when you have wheels. I zoom right into a concrete wall. I'm barely able to get my hands out in time to stop my head from getting crushed in.

I can feel Kyle's gaze as I find my balance. Quickly I realize that standing still might be harder than *moving*. So I start rolling toward the DIY dance floor as I find my center. Kyle's wheels rattle up alongside me, and suddenly I couldn't stop skating even if I wanted to.

I manage to get to the loading zone without kissing the concrete. Kyle positions her skates in a V to halt, and I do the same. We're now so close that I can feel her breath on my collarbones. Her eyes squint, as though she's about to say something she can't take back, but then she just looks away and shrugs to herself.

A few sticker dots are tangled in her hair. The light above us is flickering slowly, causing Kyle to go from starlight dancer to *shadow girl*, over and over—and I realize, she's becoming a mental stand-in for a girlfriend who probably never existed. I don't know whether to pull away or move closer, but she spins aside to fan into a figure eight.

I try to follow but end up figure *0-ing* before tumbling down onto the concrete. I get back up, quickly but gracelessly. Kyle takes a turn to spin out a complex string of shapes—figure eights, nines, whole damn alphabets—that spell out something only she can read. When it's my turn next, I barely make a full circle before sprawling on the floor again.

Kyle moves closer, ready to help me up, but something makes her waver.

"I'm okay, don't mind me," I croak.

That causes her to snort softly and my heart races.

"You're too worried about getting hurt," she whispers. "Forget about the danger and just move. It's all you can do here . . . or *anywhere*."

She utters those words like a grand secret of the universe.

Kyle zooms off to the back room's shelves. I follow after her, and we weave in and out, scratching lines in the dirty floor, round and round till we might as well be flying—and *man*, this ain't a comedown but a whole new drug fizzling inside me.

Then Kyle rolls over a power block. Tumbles. I zip over to her side, halt my skates, then reach down to grab her hand. I shiver. In my remembered life, this is the first time I've ever held hands with a girl. And whatever I'm on, *this* is the contact high.

Almost instantly Kyle tries to pull away. But I manage to

help her to her feet without letting go of her hand, and for a second, we get into a weird little tug-of-war. In doing so, we end up picking up speed and slamming into Kyle's locker on the far wall.

Her hand slips out of mine.

"Kyle. I . . . sorry, I—"

I get up and notice that her locker popped open. Atop her stuff is an open notebook with a pen sketch of something startling: four wraiths standing in front of a bright red portal.

This is an echo of my dreams! An echo of that postcard!

I spin around to find Kyle shivering, her eyes wide. She grabs her notebook and shoves it into her backpack.

"Kyle—" I barely get out both syllables before she's slammed her locker shut and is skating toward the distant exit.

"Kyle!"

I return to my apartment after dark and slump against the closed door. Lara is curled up, watching a cooking show on TV.

"Hey, dude, how was your day?" she asks, without averting her gaze from one of her crushes, master-chef David Chang.

"Uh, the usual," I murmur. "I found a pair of dentures under the racks, forgot to get breakfast cereal again, and oh, by the way, I think I'm able to see the future."

"Cool, cool," she murmurs.

I block her view of the TV, and before she can complain, I say, "You know my nightmares of four monsters emerging to cause an . . . *apoc*—" That word jams in my throat, and Lara shivers. "Kyle Kuan has also seen them."

Lara turns off the TV. "*What . . . ?*"

I tell her all about Kyle's notebook. "Kyle is seeing the same specific shit as me. That *can't* be a random coincidence, right? That *has* to mean something." My thoughts go to the nightmares themselves. "I've told you about how those dreams often feel real? Well . . . what if Kyle and I are both seeing the same future . . . with a full-blown apocalypse?"

"No, no, no, *no*," Lara interrupts, holding her paws over her ears, and I don't know if she's trying to argue with my logic or the very idea of a pending doomsday.

"Lara! *Talk to me.* You're a demon. You have to know shit. Are we heading for the full-on end of the world?"

She goes motionless as though she's pretending to be a mere plush toy.

"*Lara!*" I yell, shaking her. "Are we going to be invaded by hell?"

Lara hops out of my grip and lands on the ground beside me. "I don't want to talk about it. . . ." Before I can say anything, she looks around and says, "I know what we should do! We should move. There *must* be a nicer place out there, in a better part of the city—or even out to the burbs. Somewhere you could find some peace."

"Lara—"

The cat scampers to my laptop and uses her voice to trigger a Google search for rentals we can afford. I try to get her attention, but she's intent on changing the subject. I get up and pace, struggling to think of how to get her to focus.

"Lara, seriously, we could be facing the end of the world."

Just saying those four words fills me with a familiar dull ache. But now I realize I've been mislabeling this feeling for months: it's not tiredness, but *hopelessness*.

Suddenly all I want is to shake off this feeling. I head to my bedroom and pull out that photo of the burning dumpster. I stare at the Shadow Girl and whisper, "I wish you were here. . . . Wish you could tell me about my past . . . or how to deal with all the invisible fires *everywhere*. . . ."

I shut my eyes as my thoughts circle around the idea of *her*. Soon my head tingles, then zings, as I try to make my way above the high wall of my amnesia. But before long, I have to stop and open my eyes as I'm crushed by yet another migraine.

Burning pain flares up in my skull. But as the room swirls around me, I get another glimpse of that dumpster photo, and all I can think of is *That was real. I know it happened. That—*

My vision goes red, then white, then black, before I lose consciousness.

7

Dumpster Fire Kingdom

The next day, as I head to work, everything around me is just noise. The roadblocks. The patrollers. The only thing that snaps me out of a daze is the sight of the Vanguard asylum. I stare through the barbwire to see Doomies gathered on a distant lawn for some kind of outdoor therapy session. A counselor with a green sweater vest and curly hair is telling them to adopt different poses. (*Simon says . . . try not to lose your damn mind?*)

Keep walking. Get to work.

The mart has the two people who might just have answers: Gutierrez, who might know more about Doomies, and Kyle, who could share more of what she's seen.

Kyle. If I'm a Doomie, then so is she, right?

Man, of all the possible things we could've had in common . . .

When I enter the rear door and step into the back room, all the fluorescent lights are on. I'm blinded by the glare. I peer through my fingers to see Gully standing along the opposite wall, next to an unfamiliar Vanguard soldier who's talking quietly into her walkie-talkie. The floor looks strange in the bright light. The concrete has a creamy hue, broken by patterns of pinky red, like a strawberry ripple cheesecake that someone dropped.

Blood.

A body is lying in the middle of the room, covered with a black plastic sheet. Feet are sticking out of one end.

Oh God . . .

"Jasper!" Gully roars. "Stay back, you moron! You could end up tracking blood everywhere. Go join the others in the break room."

My body shakes as I pick a path through the puddles.

I enter the break room to see the early-shift clerks. Dean, Penelope, and Norm are preoccupied on their phones. Robbie and Jono are daring each other to drink kid's shampoo for some stupid reason. How is no one freaking out?

Our assistant manager, Marco Van Nuys, is sitting alone at a table. Dude is giant, like, nearly seven feet tall, and he's recently gotten into those adult "inner Zen" coloring books. He doodles in them whenever Gully isn't looking.

"Marco . . ."

He gives me the briefest nod. "Sup, J?"

"*Sup?* Dude, there's a—" I gesture at the distant blood. "What happened?"

Marco tells me a demon escaped the portal quarantine at 6:00 a.m. and got into the back room. Gutierrez was knocked unconscious, while Aaron Davis was badly wounded in a corner. Kyle rushed over and killed the creature, but she couldn't save Aaron from bleeding out.

I didn't actually know Aaron. We'd only exchanged brief hellos whenever we crossed paths in the back room. But still . . . fucking hell.

"Aaron is dead?"

Marco is focused back on the sunflower he's been coloring in, and I realize his hands are shaking slightly.

"Wait. Is Kyle okay? Where is she?"

"She's around here somewhere," says Marco. "Probably just waiting like the rest of us for Vanguard to come and assess whether we can open up today."

I need to see Kyle.

Gully has slipped away, so I creep out into the back room. I'm about to search for Kyle, but I freeze when a bulky guard heads my way: Aaron Davis.

Marco was mistaken.

I spin back to stare at the tarp-covered body as Aaron comes up behind me and puts a hand on my shoulder. "You knew him, right? Gutierrez."

"*Gutierrez?*"

The ground wobbles under me.

"Sorry, buddy. He seemed like a good, solid dude," Aaron mumbles, before wandering off.

A rustling draws my attention to the rear door, and I notice a kid in a green hoodie staring at Gutierrez's sheet-covered body. He inches closer and closer, until something triggers his phone to create a coin-clinking sound.

The little shit! He's the same kid who used Ollie's injuries to get compensation points. I'm about to scream at him to get the fuck out, but before I can, he's already fled the scene. And barely seconds later, two men enter through the same rear door, both dressed in white hazmat suits and black-visored helmets.

Vanguard scrubbers.

I'm frozen to my spot and can't look away.

"So much blood," one of the scrubbers mutters. "It's like a freaking oil spill."

He reaches behind him, then whips out a long hose connected to the portable vacuum cleaner that's strapped to his back. The man starts sucking up the blood from the floor. White pouches on his suit bloat up with each mechanical *slurp*.

The other scrubber joins in. Every so often, they come across bits of flesh and bone, which they store in shoulder bags.

I feel sick. I need to get away. ASAP. I dart through a door to find myself in the one staff restroom. I try to breathe steadily and distract myself with, *heck*, anything else.

This space is almost floor-to-ceiling peachy pinks, from the five stalls to the sinks and walls. Near my feet is a black helmet speckled in blood. Kyle is sitting in a corner with her knees pulled up to her chest.

Her arms are covered in blood splatter, and the bottom edge of her yellow hair is stained with red. She is trying to use her fingers to comb out her messy hair, and each shaky movement is just spreading the red around.

"Kyle?"

It's just us here.

Kyle freezes. Everything inside me settles down, as though there's only enough space in this room for one of us to fall apart—and she got here first.

I kneel beside her.

Kyle must have been a warrior angel when she slew the monster that killed Gutierrez. But now she stares ahead blankly, shivering uncontrollably. A hand-dryer is mounted on the wall behind us, so I stretch up to push the *ON* button. Hot air blasts down, and Kyle crumples into my arms. The machine makes a jet-engine roar, on and on, and I hold Kyle tightly under a cone of warmth.

When the dryer times out and stops, I ask the one thing I wish someone would ask me: "You okay?"

Kyle nods, seems to regain some calm. She gazes at my arms wrapped around her and lowers her stare as she untangles from me. Soon we sit quietly against the edge of the sinks, and she whispers, "It all happened so fast."

"What happened?"

"Aaron and Gutierrez were battling this blob with mouths—this impossible thing *made* of nothing but mouths—and Aaron got knocked unconscious. It was just Gutierrez, so . . . I . . . raced over to help him . . . but . . ." She wraps her arms around herself. "Cameron was dead before I could get to him."

Cameron Gutierrez.

I didn't even know his first name, and my grief starts to seem less like a real thing and more like a Here For You mart knockoff.

"You did your best," I tell Kyle. "You couldn't save him from—"

The restroom door swings open. A VC scrubber pokes his head in, scanning for additional blood or wreckage, as his colleague calls out from afar, "Anything in the restroom?"

"Just two F-16s," this scrubber calls out, without even settling his gaze on us. "All good."

All . . . good?

I want to stare at him, challenge him to look me in the fucking eye. But he's already gone. And before the door slides closed again, I glimpse a completely clean back room floor. Gutierrez's body is gone. Where he once lay, a plastic bag hovers and eddies, haunting the ground before floating away.

Vanguard might be the greatest cleaning company in history. Scrub, disinfect, polish, only to let shit hit the fan all over again. That's their MO. Maybe that's *all* they can do.

I exhale slowly before turning to face Kyle to say, "There's something I want to talk to you about. . . . Uh—" My mind blanks as her eyes meet mine. "Something you and I . . . We've both . . ."

Kyle stiffens but says, "You wanna talk about that now?"

"How can I ignore that sketch of yours?"

Kyle raises a brow. "*Sketch?*"

"Yeah, the sketch in your notebook. I mean . . . you're a *Doomie*, right?"

She flinches, rises to her feet. "Yeah, no. I'm not a *Doomie*."

"I didn't mean—"

And just like that, Kyle storms out of the restroom.

I try to follow her but get blocked when everyone streams into the back room. There's a buzz of excitement as a hulking Vanguard soldier with a salt-and-pepper beard and gelled-back hair strides into the center of the room. He's wearing a gray camo jacket and pants. His aviator-style sunglasses glint as he enters the fluorescent lights. His guns are holstered, one to each thigh.

Wait a sec. I'm staring at Lieutenant Davey Shiner. . . .

"Lieutenant Shiner!" Marco calls out.

Shiner takes off his sunglasses but gives a bored nod. Civilians are discouraged from taking photos of Vanguardians, but Penelope tries to sneak one. Shiner notices her, but Aaron sidles over to him and says, "Sorry, Lieutenant, I guess we're all a little starstruck." Aaron himself looks like he'd like to ask for a selfie.

Shiner pats Aaron on the shoulder and says something inaudible. Abruptly a switch goes off inside Aaron, and his cheeriness vanishes. The guard stalks over to Penelope, grabs her phone, and *hurls* it into a trash can. Penelope scurries away, tears in her eyes, and Aaron flinches as he takes in what he just did.

Gully steps over and says, "Lieutenant Shiner, I'm Gully Gorman, the manager here. I'd like to welcome you to—"

Shiner steps past Gully, for he spies someone at the back of the crowd. "You Kuan?" he asks, pointing.

Kyle steps forward, tries to straighten her shoulders, and nods.

Shiner studies her and lets out a *humph*. He gestures for her to head outside, and I notice another Vanguardian in the distance. "Head over there to be debriefed about this morning's *mess*."

"Yes, sir," says Kyle as she heads off.

Shiner gazes at the rest of us and calls out in a booming voice, "*Attention.* I don't know how many casualties you've had in this mart, but I'll remind you all that you are legally *forbidden* from discussing anything you've seen."

The staff shifts about.

Shiner's lips curl up slightly. "I'll assume you understand why, and I won't bother to explain the repercussions for violating this order. Also, in light of the recent violence, Vanguard is temporarily assigning me here for a thorough risk assessment."

Shiner finally acknowledges Gully and says he'll be taking over the store's manager office. Gully looks surprised but doesn't argue. Shiner doesn't really let him. He tells us to return to work. I'm about to try heading outside to talk to Kyle, but Shiner stalks over to me.

"*You*," he addresses me. "Who are you?"

"Jasper. Uh, can I help you with something?"

"*Humph . . .*" Shiner sizes me up, eyes narrowed. "I've seen *you* loitering outside the asylum, haven't I?"

Shit, shit, shit . . .

"Why do you—" he starts, but his walkie clicks with static. He wanders off to answer a call, and I dart back into the store. I notice Kyle heading back on her rounds, her helmet obscuring her face.

I walk over, and before Kyle can turn away, I whisper, "Look, I need to know more about your sketches, because I . . . I've seen the same things."

She falters.

So I lower my voice even more and add, "I think *I* might be a *Doomie*."

Kyle pushes up her helmet visor to look at me.

Briefly, her jaw slackens. I ask if we can talk somewhere in private, and she nods waveringly, so I lead her back into the back room, to an emptied storage closet. I close the door quietly behind us. Walls are covered in scratch marks and holes, illuminated by a single naked bulb. A demon attack occurred here ages ago, and the drywall is now all rotted due to water damage from leaky pipes.

Kyle leans back against one wall, her arms folded, while I stand against the opposite side. The vinyl floor between us might as well be an ocean of black and white squares.

"Why do you think you're a *Doomie*?" she asks.

"It's a few things. I have recurring nightmares about four ghostlike creatures who touch a portal and cause it to gush an apocalypse horde. . . . And then there's my amnesia—"

"Wait. *What?*"

"My amnesia. I thought you knew?"

I assumed *everyone* here knew.

"You've got amnesia? For real?"

"Yeah . . . I can't remember anything except for, like, the past few months."

Kyle takes off her helmet and drops it to cause an enormous *thunk*, Kevlar on concrete. Next thing I know, she's laughing like she's just heard the greatest joke ever—like *I'm* the greatest joke ever.

"Kyle. I don't see what's funny. Either I'm going crazy, or the world is ending, or both those things are happening!"

Kyle sees my face redden and hushes. "No, I didn't mean to laugh. It's just . . ." She wavers, leans forward to cause her yellow hair to curtain her face. "I just, when we met again at the mart, I thought you were ignoring me . . . and I was fucking mad. I . . ."

Kyle wraps her arms around herself, and a sudden soberness makes it hard to read her expression as she says quietly, "Listen, I want to tell you . . ."

When I step closer, she stiffens and clears her throat.

"I just never would've guessed you were a Doomie.

You . . . see the same glimpses of the future?"

I nod. "But how do you know it's the future?"

Her brows crease as she studies me. "Well . . . I can sometimes *sense* when monsters are about to emerge. Every now and then, just before an attack, I get a gut feeling that something bad is right around the corner." Her shoulders tense up. "Whenever I get nightmares of the apocalypse, I get that *exact* gut feeling—only amped up to a ten."

My eyes widen. "Rewind a sec. You can *sense* the coming of monsters?"

"Sometimes," she replies. "It's something that's helped me save a few people as a VC trainee. But . . ." Her eyes gaze at her helmet to take in a huge new scratch. "But despite sensing that something was coming today, I just couldn't—"

"It's not your fault," I interrupt, wandering over to rest my shoulders beside hers. "You know that, right?"

Silence.

"Maybe if we work together, we can learn more about the apocalypse stuff, decipher these nightmares, and somehow find a way to . . ."

I can't say it, but I'm thinking: *save the world.*

"*Do something.*"

"Do something? We can barely survive this place on a bad day, and you want to . . ." Kyle sinks slowly down the wall, gaze glassy, and an invisible string tugs me down with her. "Hell itself punched *holes* in our world. How do you fight a force that powerful?"

"I . . . don't know."

But crouching beside her, at least I know I'm no longer alone in all this.

Her gaze is focused on the opposite wall, where the soaked drywall has a hole at the bottom edge, revealing rotted plywood. The hole breaches two layers. I can see light from the alley outside.

I walk over there and kick the hole wider. Let in more light.

Kyle moves over, raises a brow at me.

I say, "Sure, we barely survive on bad days. Heck, we barely get by on the good days, when all we do is work jobs that don't matter, buy shit we don't need, and watch cat videos in bed until our bloodshot eyes roll back in our fuckin' skulls. But still—" I punch a shoulder-level hole in the wall. "We're not powerless to make holes of our own. Plans of our own. *Something*." I lean against the wall. Pat it. "Come on."

Kyle looks away, snorts softly. Then without warning, she punches the space right next to my head. I flinch. But when her eyes glimmer, I find myself grinning like an idiot.

We turn our attention to that lowermost hole and crouch to tear away more of the drywall. Soon we've got enough room to reach through the wall and rip away at the outermost layer of soggy board, until finally, we push our feet to this hole and kick the edges wider and wider.

Eventually, we're half in the room, half out, our feet in the alley. I'm panting. She's panting. Our legs are touching.

Hips too. I feel self-conscious that my breathing is *way* too loud.

Kyle's gaze settles on me, and we might as well be in that TV show in my head called *PORTALS*. Only this time there's no laugh track, and damn, our *Will they or won't they?* vibes are starting to feel pretty real. Or maybe that's just my imagination.

But somehow, I have the fucking audacity to not look away. Instead, I whisper, "This apocalypse—if we don't try to push it back, kick it in the nuts hard—it'll keep pushing us around."

A smile creeps over her face. "Do you seriously suggest we should just kick the apocalypse in the nuts?"

"Hell yeah!" I shout, and then like some kind of deranged war cry, I chant, *"In the nuts! In the nuts!"*

Kyle starts laughing. "Okay, okay!" She holds a hand over my mouth, and her touch makes me freeze. Almost as quickly, she pulls away and shifts her eyeline. "I have an idea."

Out we go, through the hole and into the alley beyond. It's a narrow corridor with an overflowing dumpster. Guards aren't supposed to throw monster waste in the general garbage, but I can literally see a mutant lizard tail draped over the edge of the bin. Although Kyle is several steps away, our shadows appear side by side on the ground, silhouetted hands connected—

"You really don't remember anything of your past?"

Kyle asks, and I turn to face her. "What's the first thing you remember?"

Her scrutiny makes me feel like a freak.

I shrug. "What's *your* first memory?"

Kyle shrugs. "Believe it or not, I remember being in the hospital, like, as a newborn baby. White lights and shit."

"Same! Except . . . I wasn't being born. It was just me waking up in the hospital after my accident."

Kyle gestures at the scummy alley and says with a snort, "Hah! In that case, welcome to your fantastic, wonderful world, baby!" Though we're only joking, hearing her say *baby*—right to my face—makes my cheeks grow warm.

"So. This idea of yours?" I ask before the warm turns to a full blush.

"Right. You remember Pete Moretti?"

"Pete? Yeah, he was a clerk here, until two months ago when he quit."

Pete was weird. Tall dude with a bowl haircut dyed green, who used to buy *tons* of the mart's clothing after each shift. (Like, seriously, who needs polyester shirts that come in a reusable ziplock bag?) I didn't know him well, but he was one of the few clerks who didn't give me a dumb nickname.

"Pete didn't quit," says Kyle. "VC flagged him as a possible Doomie."

"I had no idea. . . ."

"I was tasked to bring him to the VC asylum for an eval. But I just couldn't dump him there. Pete's a good guy. So, I brought him here." Kyle gestures at a broken security camera in a corner and says, "This is a CCTV blind spot here. I told Pete to run, and I later told Vanguard that Pete shoved me down and took off."

I don't know what to say.

"I don't know much about Doomies—no one outside the VC asylum and med staff really do—but Pete's Doomsday Delirium seemed bad. I've got a definite feeling he's seen *way* more future shit than we have."

"Do you know where he is now?"

Kyle nods, then looks at her watch, and I realize it's almost my break time, and maybe hers too. "I do. But trigger warning—" She leans in closer. "There might be *blood*."

8

Bloody Big
Discounts

I don't know where we're headed, but the streets on the way are strangely empty of roadblocks. Kyle gazes back at me as we cross an empty intersection, and the invisible barriers around her also seem to have vanished. And damn, I don't know what to do with all the *space* between us.

I stop in my tracks, and we halt on an empty street corner. We're alone, and I mutter, "So . . . How did you, y'know, become a Doomie?"

Kyle rolls her shoulders. "I don't know. I'd been having the same nightmare over and over . . . sharper and clearer . . . and one day I realized my life had changed."

"Changed how?"

Kyle shrugs and gazes at the distance. "Doomsday Delirium disconnects you from everything. Makes you seem like a stranger to everyone, even yourself." She side-eyes me. "So. Amnesia. What's that like?"

No one's ever asked me that. "It's hard to explain. Like, have you ever bought a piece of clothing from the mart? You know how after it gets washed, it just stretches and shrinks and warps into something unwearable? Well, that's my life. Nothing about it seems to really fit like it should anymore. Does that make any sense?"

Kyle shrugs and says, "As much as anything does anymore."

"It's like I'm always searching for myself. I used to wander around the city, hoping to stumble into someone I recognized—" I hush as Kyle gazes into my eyes, longer than I remember *anyone* ever looking at me.

Kyle seems ready to say something, but her invisible roadblocks slide back out as she frowns instead. "There it is," she says, pointing at something behind me.

Kyle hurries ahead, guiding me to a rundown building with no signage. I follow her through an open entrance, then down to the basement, where we find ourselves in front of sliding doors that are painted solid black. Stenciled in bright red letters are the words: *BLOODY BIG DISCOUNTS*.

I cock a brow at Kyle. "Ominous much?"

We step toward the doors, but they won't open. Instead, my phone's VC app shows me a legal notice: **Store management is not responsible for health issues that might arise from the use of affected products....**

Before I can read it all, Kyle reaches over and presses *ACCEPT* on my phone, and the doors slide open. What I see is a moldy ceiling with naked bulbs. Unpainted walls with signs like NO CHANGEROOMS and NO REFUNDS OR RETURNS. The store is half the size of the Here For You, and instead of aisles and shelves, this store organizes its inventory into huge mounds. It's mostly clothes. Clothes splattered with bloodstains and vomit and other viscera, both human and demon. The whole place stinks of it.

It takes me a long moment to find my voice.

"So. Something tells me we're *not* the target demographic of this place." I turn to find Kyle covering her nose. "What is this joint?"

Kyle gestures around us. "VC figured it was wasteful for stores to incinerate bloodstained goods. So they created 'monster-damaged apparel' stores—MDAs. You can purchase stuff here by the pound."

"Seriously? How come people don't talk about this?" I ask.

"Well, there's *this*." Kyle tries to take a pic of the store, but her phone cam shows a gray blur. "And, of course, none of the 'regulars' are gonna blab about MDAs." She gestures at two old ladies who are grabbing as many baby bibs as they can from a pile of blood-speckled fabric. They eye each other warily, and you'd think they were competing over gold.

All this chaos, and not even a portal in sight . . . !

"A week ago, I saw Pete enter here wearing a work vest," says Kyle.

"Great sleuthing, Scoob," I joke as we wander through the mounds. A second later we catch sight of the checkouts, where only three of the seven registers are manned. My gaze goes to a green-haired dude behind register one.

Bingo.

Pete is bobbing around as he places several bloodstained bikinis on a large scale. He addresses the shopper (an old guy wearing a business shirt and boxer shorts): "All righty! That weighs four pounds, mister! So, that'll be four dollars, please." Pete sets a little packet atop the mound and adds, "Please enjoy your complimentary Tide laundry pod."

The man hands Pete four bucks, grabs the bikinis, then ambles away.

"Come again soon!" Pete calls out with a smile—an actual bright *smile*.

There's no one else in the line, so we head over to Pete. I wave politely and call out, "Uh, hey, Pete. Remember us?"

"Jasper? What are you—"

Pete freaks out when he sees Kyle's Kevlar vest—and its yellow text that reads *VANGUARD*. He yelps and seems ready to bolt.

But Kyle holds out her hands and says, "Pete. It's me. Kyle."

"*Kyle?*" He takes in her face, calms a little, but still looks uneasy. "Kyle. Hey, you . . . you shouldn't be here." He looks left and right, but we're out of earshot of anyone else. "How did you even find me?"

Kyle moves closer to him. "We just need a minute, man. We wanna talk about those visions you had of the four ghostly monsters of the . . . well, *apocalypse*."

Pete swallows hard. "Apoc . . . apoc . . . apo . . ." He squeezes his eyes shut. "Apo . . . apologies! I can't help you with that, so, er, have a nice day and come again some other time."

Pete tries to slip away, but Kyle blocks his path. "Pete,

you can trust us. We're not going to tell Vanguard anything. In fact, we just want to know about the apoca—"

"Nup, nup, nup!" he mutters, plugging his ears with his fingers. "None of that here, folks!"

Pete flees the checkout and zips between mounds of clothing. But just as we trail after him, he slips on a sock, trips, and slams face-first into a towering mound of clothes. Kyle and I look at each other, like *What have we done?* as we slowly approach his suddenly motionless body.

"Uh. Pete? You okay?" Kyle whispers once before taking another step closer and asking again.

Abruptly, Pete stirs and stretches out his arms—as though to *hug* the mound—and we hear him whisper, "It's okay, it's okay, it's okay." Is he talking to himself? Or the *clothes*? Pete rolls over and exhales. He catches sight of a metallic bomber jacket lying at his feet and lets out a long *Ooh!* "Where did you come from, buddy?"

Pete grabs the jacket, then wanders over to a nearby basket labeled STAFF USE.

Kyle and I approach. Pete stiffens when he notices us again, but I quickly tell him, "Pete, I'm sorry if we freaked you out. We just—"

"I—I don't want to talk about that, *that* stuff," he stammers.

I don't know what to do, but I don't want him to bolt, so I nod. "Sure, dude. We don't have to talk about that stuff. Um . . ." I focus on Pete himself. "Let's start over. How are you actually doing, man?"

Pete eyes us warily, but I smile, and that settles him a

little. "Um. I'm *good*." He shifts about uneasily, until his gaze settles on the jacket in his hands, and instantly his mood brightens. "Definitely good today, considering the awesome finds I've snagged. I mean, look at this beauty! Whaddaya think?"

I stare at the bloodstains on the cuffs of both sleeves. "Uh, it's . . . a little worse for wear?"

"*Eh*. A little blood never hurt nobody. I can't believe I didn't see this during first dibs."

"*Pete*," Kyle begins.

I can sense Kyle getting impatient, so I flash her a look that I hope says, *Hold on*, before turning to Pete to try to keep him talking. "What's 'first dibs'?"

"Oh, just the *coolest thing* about this job. Each morning, before the crowds enter, us staff get first dibs to buy the best stuff that comes here. You'll never believe the amazing things I've found in this joint!" He pats his chest, and I realize he's wearing multiple T-shirts and two jackets under his work vest. How is he not sweltering? "This job is incredible!"

Okay, yeah . . . Pete's definitely gotten a *lot* crazier since we last met.

Then again, I guess the same is probably true for me. So before Pete can be distracted by any more bargains, I move closer to say, "Look, Pete. I know what it's like to be a little . . . not normal. That's actually why we're here."

"Not normal?" Pete echoes. "Are you okay?"

"Not me—" I begin, but then I realize there *is* a question he could help with. "Actually, I never got the chance to ask you this, but what do you remember of me from, like, before my accident?"

Pete frowns slightly, shrugging. "Uh. You mostly just kept to yourself."

I sigh. "Yeah, someone else told me the same thing recently."

"Oh, I do remember one thing. You were always friendly— quiet but friendly—but a few weeks before your accident, you just . . . became like a *zombie*. You changed into a lifeless shell of a person."

This! My Doomsday Delirium catalyst!

"Do you know what caused this change?" I ask, holding my breath.

Pete shrugs. "Sorry. I had a lot of my own shit to deal with. I wasn't paying that close attention."

Sighing, I focus back on why we came here today. "Pete," I admit, "I think I'm a Doomie. I think Kyle's one too." His eyes widen as I explain how Kyle and I have both seen similar nightmares. Pete gets antsy again, but at least he doesn't dart away. "Look, I know I said we didn't need to talk about that stuff, but damn, we really *do*."

"Why?" He retreats a step.

"So we can . . ." I struggle to finish that sentence, until Kyle steps over to my side, and I add, "Maybe try to save this dump of a world of ours."

Pete stares at the ground for a long moment, then finally sighs and says, "I *have* seen a lot of things that maybe most

Doomies haven't. But if I make myself think of those things, I'll probably have a total breakdown. I can't, man. I just can't."

"But if we can stop what's coming, maybe we can get you right again—"

"Look, dudes," he tells us, holding up his hands. "I just want to live my life, do what I love, and be around my *friends*." He pats his clothes at that last word, and I get this weird sense that maybe he's talking about what he's wearing. "Why should I try to change something that can't be changed?"

"You don't think we can stop the . . . end?" Kyle whispers.

Pete shakes his head. "I just . . . just . . ." He crouches down as he clutches his head tightly and shudders. "No, no, no, no . . . can't go there, Pete. Can't!"

I kneel beside him and put a hand on his shoulder. "I . . . I'm sorry. This was a mistake to come here. We'll find another way—"

Pete sucks in a breath and grabs my arm shakily. I halt as he mutters, "I didn't say I wouldn't help." He sits cross-legged and flicks a gaze between Kyle and me. "But I want something in return."

Kyle scoots over to crouch beside us and asks warily, "What?"

"I need 160,000 VC points," says Pete with a surprising directness. "Exactly 160,000 cold, hard points delivered straight to my VC app within the half hour."

"*Seriously?*" I ask, before Kyle adds, "That's a tall order, dude."

Pete pulls out his phone and opens an unfamiliar app called Vanguard Sales Assistance. He clicks a confidentiality waiver, then gets to a long list of items for sale—antiques, cars, artwork, along with bulk lots of cheaper items. Unlike the MDA, most of this stuff seems to be in good condition.

"Is this like Vanguard's secret version of eBay?" I ask.

Kyle does a double take. "*Oh.* I know what this is." She averts her gaze from me as she says, "Uh, so . . . yeah, a lot of people on Hell Portal Day . . ."

"Died?" I whisper.

Kyle nods. "Yes. And because of that, there was a lot of stuff left behind. Vanguard tries to relocate stuff to a deceased's next of kin, but when there's no one to claim anything, Vanguard stores the stuff in secret warehouses. And I *think* they use this app to do, like, estate sales."

My gaze returns to the app's listings. "This is *all* from Hell Portal Day?"

"It might be years till they've processed everything," she mumbles.

I think of my parents' furniture and books. Is this where those items would have ended up if I weren't still here? Would their stuff just be bundled into a bulk lot of other people's junk? My fists clench as I ask, "Pete. *Why* are you showing us this?"

Pete is once again chipper, and I want to shake him, hard. Doesn't he see the horror all around him? But he just opens one listing in particular: A bulk lot of unclaimed designer goods. Hundreds of pieces of (mostly) undamaged jackets, shoes, shirts that come in both men's and women's sizes. "So. I need 160,000 VC points to buy this lot. It expires in twenty-eight minutes."

"That's, like, eight thousand dollars," Kyle hisses.

I exhale. Focus. "Right." I open my VC app, click on the wallet section, then read aloud my balance: "I've got 10,001 VC points."

Kyle opens her VC app to show me 11,800 VC. "That means we're short almost 140,000 points." She pauses. "I have about thirty-five hundred dollars that I could convert from cash to VC points. You?"

"I've got about twenty-five hundred dollars in my bank account."

Kyle uses the calculator on her phone: "At a conversion rate of twenty VC points to a dollar . . ." She lets out a huff. "Shit. We'll still be short 18,200 VC."

"It's all or nothing," says Pete.

When we waver, he seems ready to head off.

"Okay, okay! Just give us a few minutes," says Kyle. "Let us try to pull it together."

Pete wanders off to give us space.

That's when Kyle looks at the shoppers milling about and frowns. "Humph." She gets to her feet, and so do I. "Hey, can you bring out the worst in these shoppers?"

"Worse than this?" I gesture at the bikini-buying guy, who has come back to grab some bloodied luggage—presumably for some terrifying holiday he's going on.

"I need you to bring out the *absolute* worst," she tells me.

"Well, okay, then. I'll do my best."

There are only four clerks working, and no manager is in sight. When no one is looking, I sneak behind the info counter and reach for the intercom. I'm about to make an announcement, but I freeze when I think of why I always dodge the public speaking stuff. Public speaking requires you to put yourself out there, but what if you don't know *who* you really are? But then Kyle gives me a wink and a smile, and suddenly I become . . .

THE. MOTHER. FUCKING. GUY.

"Attention, shoppers! How y'all doing today in fair *Sundownnn Cityyyy*?"

Cringe overload. I sound like a deranged radio announcer.

Kyle raises a brow.

I redden but continue: "*Well, well, well, folks!* For the next five minutes, everything in the aisle—I mean the, uh, mound near the door—is free of charge. You heard me, people! Free, free, free! You'd have to be *caaaa-razy* to miss out! I repeat, everything there is free! Bibs! Cribs! Claim your dibs!"

I scuttle away just in time to see mounds of clothes wobble like Jell-O as shoppers rush to the "mound near the door." People are cheering and, soon, yelling as they fight over crumpled clothes.

Finally, a manager in a polo shirt gets on the PA to say

that the "sale" was a prank. But it's too late.

The mounds of blood-dirtied clothes tumble to the floor. Fists start flying. Kyle darts over and hops up onto a large carton. She pulls out a whistle from her Kevlar vest, then blows out a painfully sharp note. People freeze, look up at the word *Vanguard* on her attire.

Kyle hops down and calls out, "Under directive eighty-nine of Vanguard's city regulation rules, I hereby dock all your VC accounts of two thousand points each for disorderly conduct."

The nearest guy lumbers over and casts a huge shadow around her as he says, "I ain't takin' orders from a pocket-sized *trainee*."

Kyle doesn't even blink. "My mistake. Twenty-five hundred VC points."

He wavers, but she stares him down witheringly.

"Fine!" he hisses, stepping backward.

Kyle gestures for them to line up. "Phones. Present your VC apps. *Now*."

Ten dudes open their VC apps and take turns handing their phones to her. Moments later, Kyle has pushed buttons in each account, and they've wandered off. I head to her side, and she discreetly shows me her VC app, which has twenty-five thousand extra points.

"Wow," I mutter.

"Instead of deducting the points, I used their phones to initiate a transfer to my account," says Kyle. "With any luck, they'll never notice it went to *me* and not VC. But even if they do . . . well, we have more important things to worry about, right?"

We go over to Pete. Transfer 160,000 VC points to him. His face lights up as he presses a button within the sales app to buy those designer clothes. "Dudes! *Thank you, thank you, thank you!*" he exclaims as he reaches out to squish us both with a hug.

Pete leads us to the store's back room. We enter a small closet, and he closes it behind us before flicking on a bulb. He takes in a breath before mumbling, "Fire away. What do you want to know?"

I can't help it. I ask how he became a Doomie.

"Well, I'd known about the Doomies for a while. One of my neighbors was a Doomie. I thought he was crazy. But one day, there was a monster in the mart—a humanoid guy made of matchsticks—that broke through the portal quarantine and got into the aisles. I think this was before your accident, Jasper."

"What happened?" Kyle asks.

"The monster walked up to me and actually *spoke*. It said to me, '*Doomed . . . Everything is doomed*,' and then touched my arm. It singed my skin there." Pete shows us a scar on his forearm that resembles a series of lines. "The whole experience freaked me out . . . and my mind just cracked open. Broke."

Kyle looks closer at his scar. "That almost looks like a . . . *barcode?*"

Pete leads us out of the closet and over to a

product-scanning station, which would've been used before this place became an MDA. He sticks his forearm under the laser, and the machine translates his barcode scar into a "product" description:

The end. 11/29/2024. A783.

I freeze. "The end? As in . . ."

"You-know-what," says Pete, narrowing his eyes in concentration, as though struggling to stay focused on the present. "*A783* is a mystery . . . but the date . . . I think that's when it happens."

I recognize the date from the memos posted by Gully.

"A *Black Friday* apocalypse?" Kyle and I breathe.

It's like the worst promotional tie-in ever—retail hell meets *actual* hell!

"We need to report this to VC!" I interrupt. "Like, ASAP!"

Pete regains enough focus to say: "I already did that. I phoned one of their helplines and told them about the monster and the barcode. . . . I was scared, and I made the mistake of telling them about my hallucinations."

"That's how they flagged you as a Doomie," says Kyle.

"Wait. So VC flagged you instead of calling you in to ask you about what you saw? How can they not see the danger?" I ask.

Kyle folds her arms and exhales. "They don't want to panic the public. I think they see the danger, but they've gotten cocky." She tells us that VC is adding more guards to portal zones in the lead-up to Black Friday. "They probably believe they're powerful enough to stop a potential doomsday attack—and that doing so will be great PR."

Pete slumps against a wall before adding, "Listen, ever since that day with the barcode monster, I've had dreams of a Black Friday *event*. . . . Four ghostlike figures gather at a portal and, somehow, just trigger it into gushing monsters. More monsters than you've ever, ever seen. I've had that vision a thousand times."

"Yeah," Kyle whispers, "we've seen it too."

He takes in a breath. "Right. But a few nights ago, I had a *different* dream. I saw the moment when these four ghostlike figures *first* entered our world weeks ago. I saw them wandering around, unseen by everyone, as they checked us out. They spoke to one another . . . and although I didn't understand their language . . . I got a sense of who they actually are."

When he's silent, I ask, "Who are they?"

Pete takes in a breath. "They're the horsemen."

"The horsemen, as in . . . the horsemen of the apocalypse?" I ask.

"Like from the Bible?" Kyle adds.

When Pete nods, Kyle and I swap a wide-eyed look.

Pete says, "I think they each represent a dark energy. Like, one of them embodies psychotic *rage*, and he can touch people to make them go apeshit. Another one is a bully who can imprison people with his touch."

"They have *powers*?" Kyle asks.

"Right. *Of course* they'd have powers," I mutter.

"That's not all—" He seems to lose track of that sentence briefly. "I can't explain it . . . but I have this feeling that the horsemen *won't* be ghostly figures on Black Friday. Somehow I think they're now trying to become . . . *solid*." Pete shudders, holds out a hand to shield himself from something only he can see, and mutters, "No, no, no!"

"*Pete.* Stay with us." I hold on to his shoulders and try to get him to breathe. "Pete? You're hallucinating. Listen to my voice."

Right then, a deep rumbling echoes in the distance. The ground shakes. Kyle and I carefully help Pete to a seat nearby before we rush to a back door to peer outside.

"What's happening?" I ask as we step out onto the street.

"I don't know," Kyle whispers. "But that does not sound good."

A few blocks ahead, the street leads into a park, where there's an outdoor portal that's shaking and rumbling within a quarantine cage. Nearby families stagger up from their picnic blankets and start darting away. Pigeons take to the sky.

But then, the rumbling gives way to a thunderous boom, and a chunk of rock shoots out from the portal and through the cage bars. The rock soars up a hundred feet before arcing back down to earth. It smashes onto the grass and bursts into a dense cloud of gray dust. In a split second, the park vanishes under this heavy fog, and seconds later, so too do nearby buildings, streets, and—

Shit! Run!

9

Dystopian Delight

VC Klaxons roar. Kyle and I retreat to the MDA only to find the exit door locked behind us.

"We have to take cover!" Kyle yells as she guides me quickly across the street, stopping traffic, and over to a Baskin-Robbins.

We barely make it inside as people push in along with us. The store is already well beyond capacity by the time the clerk locks the doors behind the last person, and we all stare out the windows as a wall of gray rushes down the street, blocking out everything. Even the sun becomes a faint blur.

"What's going on?" I whisper to Kyle.

"Brimstone."

My gaze takes in the gap between door panels, where a thin line of gray is seeping through, filling the air with the smell of ash and cigarettes.

Brimstone.

Every now and then, random portals occasionally shoot out chunks of superdense carbon. When these "brimstone" chunks hit solid ground, they powderize into dense clouds of ash.

"I think it's just one chunk," says Kyle.

"That's all from *one* chunk?"

Over the next few minutes, the brimstone spreads and slows. But many of the folks who made it into the Baskin-Robbins are choking from the ash. Someone clicks an asthma inhaler. Kids are crying. In front of us, there's a young girl with a My Little Pony backpack that features four horses—and all I can think is *The My Little Ponies of the Apocalypse.*

But then my attention shifts outside, as several figures stalk through the fog-clouded street. They move with an eerie calm, unaffected by the dust—and I shudder when I count *four* individuals.

They're now trying to become . . . solid.

"That can't be . . . ," Kyle whispers, her shoulder pressed against mine, shivering.

One of the figures spies us huddled together in this ice cream shop. He halts, and I let out a huge sigh as I realize it's just a VC soldier with a gas mask and a megaphone.

"It's all right, folks!" he calls out. The other soldiers help a pair of coughing pedestrians, handing them masks and guiding them to safety. "Attention, everyone. This is a temporary lockdown. Please wait indoors until the VC app gives you the all clear to return outside. Vanguard thanks you for your cooperation."

The soldiers continue down the street.

My racing heart slows, and my adrenaline starts to fade. The world isn't ending right this moment. But I start to dwell on what Pete shared. If he's right, the horsemen are literal beings, out in the world, doing shit right now.

I sink into a crouch. A hopelessness scampers down from my head to my heart, and then reaches back up to wrap its tendrils around my shoulders and press its heavy, cold head against my neck.

Kyle's huddled beside me, and I *know* I can't become some limp, useless shell. I have to help her even if it suddenly feels so pointless.

Chiming sounds flood the store. I pull out my phone to see the message: **While you wait, Vanguard would like to offer you 200 VC points and a special gift.** The latter is a coupon for a free Baskin-Robbins single scoop. (Toppings are extra.)

People start flowing toward the store register, and Kyle and I follow. What else are we going to do? Five minutes later, I'm huddled in the corner next to a plastic potted plant, eating a Mango Tango with rainbow sprinkles. (Yeah, I paid extra for them.)

I take a few licks and then toss the rest into the plant. "Mango Tango is kind of gross."

"Then why'd you order it?" she asks, finishing her snack by biting the bottom of the cone and sucking the ice cream out.

I shrug. "I'm always trying unfamiliar flavors, to see

what I might've once liked. Or hated. Call it a voyage of self-discovery." I look over at the menu board. "I've tried about half the thirty-one flavors already." My gaze flicks to a calendar next to the menu and the few days left till Black Friday. "Ergo the Mango Tango."

Kyle is gazing at an empty corner of the store, where brimstone particles are coalescing into gray snowflakes. I lean in closer and whisper, "Look. We should try to figure out what to do next, y'know, about . . . the *horsemen*."

When Kyle doesn't respond, I shift to face the same direction.

"Maybe we should . . ." My words peter out. "Look, I honestly don't know *what* we're supposed to do."

Kyle stares at VC workers outside who are spraying water, and her expression flattens as she whispers, "Maybe we've *already* been struck by an apocalypse and people just don't wanna acknowledge that." Her eyes meet mine, and she purses her lips. "That's . . ."

"Kyle?"

"Just . . . something my ex-boyfriend used to say."

"Is that what *you* believe?"

Her eyeline lowers as she picks a pebble from her boot sole. The VC logos on her footwear make me ask, "Why did you even become a VC trainee, then?"

Kyle freezes for a long moment before sighing softly. "Last year . . . my ex and I nearly died in a demon attack in the subway. Afterward, I decided to join Vanguard . . .'cause

I didn't want to be afraid anymore."

"Did your ex join you?" I ask.

"No. He was so disillusioned that he started getting obsessed with the Suckerpunch hackers and all their conspiracy theories." Her gaze locks on the grimy floor. "I used to wish he'd snap out of it, get his shit together. But now . . . after seeing how Pete loses himself in his work, I think maybe *I'm* using my own job to distract me from"—she pulls her knees to her chest, finally gazing at me—"just how pointless it is to even *try* to fix what's been broken."

"Kyle." I shift closer. "I know what it's like to feel that things are just forever hopeless. I work in the armpit of the city. I can't seem to get my memories back, and nothing really makes sense." I gently place a hand on her shoulder. "But didn't we decide to *do something*?"

Kyle shifts away from my grip to face me. "That's just it. We're not *doing* anything. . . . We're just darting from one battle to another, sidestepping one blood puddle after another. We're just dancing in the chaos."

She gets to her feet.

But I rise and say, "*Fine*. Just because we're dancing doesn't mean we can't make a difference." I reach out for her hand, curl her fingers into a fist, and wrap my palm around it. "Hell, we've *already* started something here, and we can't stop now. I gotta believe some things are worth fighting for."

The fact that we've somehow become a *we* is fucking unbelievable.

Kyle straightens her shoulders.

"Why d'you even want to save this world?" she asks, gaze sharpening.

"Why not? I'm always looking for a fun, low-cost hobby," I reply, smiling. "And heck, it might just be how I stop being a total nobody."

The corners of her lips curl up slightly, and she pushes harder against my palm. Enough that I stagger back slightly. "You're not a nobody." We lower our hands, and she adds, "But you're definitely not who I thought you were."

I don't know what she means, but I can't help but wonder: "In school . . . were we friends?"

She looks at me long and hard, but before she can answer, our VC apps chime with a new message: **You may vacate your current location, provided you do not suffer from an acute respiratory condition. Have a nice day.**

The Baskin-Robbins starts emptying, and brimstone-heavy air rushes in. Soon, it's just as foggy inside as it is out, so we step out onto the wet sidewalk, where the dampened ash looks like gray chocolate. A flavor that I'm naming Dystopian Fudge.

Kyle joins me in staring at the still-falling sky and says, "Vanguard might secretly know something about the horsemen. Obviously we can't just ask them, but there *is* a group that knows a lot about Vanguard's secrets." She lowers her voice to a whisper. "*Suckerpunch.*"

I raise a brow, and she adds, "Hear me out. Those

Suckerpunch hackers somehow discovered I allowed Pete to escape, and they tried to recruit me. Obviously I said no. But . . . they could be useful right now."

"Do you know how to contact them?"

"I think so."

Kyle nearly slips on the wet ash. I grab her hand, steady her, and she shivers slightly before gently pulling away. I'm reminded again of the strange energy between us.

"Kyle. Tell me the truth: Did I do something to upset you that I can't remember? I have this weird sense that I fucked something up."

We halt. Kyle looks at the ground as she scrapes ash with her boots. "Right . . . *that*. I'm sorry for being all weird. You remember when I joined the mart?"

That was two weeks after my accident.

I'd spotted Kyle standing in aisle three, and her yellow hair drew my attention with such suddenness. I found myself heading over to say hello and introduce myself.

Kyle shrugs. "I guess I was upset that you forgot me."

"So we *were* friends," I reply, and that simple thought is bewildering.

Motion emerges as an ash-covered man darts down the opposite sidewalk. "It's coming, people! Wake up! The apocalypse is just round the corner!" he calls out.

It's Pete.

Kyle and I call out his name, but he doesn't even see us, lost in a state of hysteria.

Right then, a VC soldier darts over, pins him against a wall, and Pete screams even louder, "It's coming!"

Another soldier arrives and helps his colleague pull Pete into a nearby VC van.

Kyle calls out, "Wait! Hold on!"

She tries to jostle her way through the pedestrians to stop the guards, but she's too late. Pete has been tossed inside the back of the van. My heart is pounding as I stand beside Kyle and can't do anything but watch the van pull away.

"Damn Doomies," says a passing stranger. "We don't need more nutjobs."

"Fuck off!" I tell the guy, shoving him.

He flinches, thinks about pushing back, but then wanders away.

"They're taking him to the asylum. We have to stop them!"

Kyle looks into the distance, shakes her head. "We can't. There's no way to free him."

My stomach twists as I whisper, "Pete's getting locked up, and it's our fault."

Kyle steps in front of me. "We had no choice."

I want to argue that maybe we could have found another info source, but she moves closer to whisper: "Besides, we've got bigger fish to fry. If we somehow stop the apocalypse, doing so *might* help all the Doomies begin to heal. Including Pete."

I don't know if Kyle believes this, but she doesn't look away.

"We can do this, *Jasper*. We have to do this."

This is the first time she's *ever* spoken my name—well, that I can remember—and she utters it like a promise that things will somehow be okay.

I take in a deep breath. Try to momentarily put aside thoughts of Pete.

"Let's head away from all this mud," Kyle whispers, only to then pause. "Uh, hey . . . Aren't we supposed to be, like, at *work* right now?"

"Oh, right," I reply.

Not even the apocalypse can shake us free of our pointless jobs. That thought makes me laugh, like it's the punch line to our stupid lives.

Kyle, too, chuckles as we head for the mart. We travel down sidewalks where wet ash has dried and cracked in the hot air to resemble old, broken pottery. We hush as we squeeze through crowds, so close that we bump elbows, and the chaos finally seems to work in my favor.

Until we get to the Here For You mart.

As we approach the store's rear loading zone, we see a couple of workers carrying out crates from a supply truck. Kyle and I crash to a halt when we notice a crate just a few feet away.

The box has a store-specific label stuck to its side: *A783*.

"A783, that's the number on Pete's . . ." Kyle clams up.

All I want to do is cry out, *Holy shit!* But after a long pause I whisper, "Of course it's gonna unfold here." This is completely and totally *on-brand*. Satan's a marketing genius.

Kyle reaches for my hand, gently unfolding my fingers that I realize were digging into my palm. She squeezes tightly. And, man, if she'd allow me, I would never let go—

But then she pulls away to whip out her phone. "I'm sending Suckerpunch a message." As she starts typing, I realize there's a resource of my own that I have yet to tap. After Kyle presses *SEND*, she says, "Suckerpunch might take a while to respond. What now?"

I look at the mart and ask, "Can you ditch work early today?"

When she asks why, I reply, "Okay, so, there's a demon *situation* you should see."

Her eyes widen. "Uh . . . *What?*"

10

Psychological Garbage Juice

I made Kyle swear not to summon VC no matter what and told her I'd answer her questions when we got to my apartment. But now that we're outside my front door, I can see the hesitation in her eyes. I take a breath, and as we enter the apartment, I say, "So, when you meet her—"

Kyle blinks. "Her?"

"Just keep an open—"

But before I can finish my thought, I'm interrupted by Lara, who saunters out from her favorite napping spot behind the TV and says, "Hey, J. Did you remember to get guacamole—"

Kyle's training kicks in, and she pulls her dagger. I have to step between her and Lara so no one gets stabbed.

"That's the *demon*?" Kyle hisses.

"That's my *roommate*—Lara," I reply. "Yes, she's a demon. But she's also harmless! Trust me. *Please.*"

"*Jasper*—"

"Kyle. Not everything is what it seems," I whisper, stepping closer to gently lower her dagger.

Lara pokes her head between my legs to peer up at Kyle.

"Uh, hey there?" Lara chirps.

Kyle exhales shakily but puts away her weapon.

I get them to sit on the couch with me, Kyle to my left, Lara to my right. I proceed to explain how I came across Lara and that she's an anomalous, pacifist demon. I tell Kyle, "Lara can help us with our mission."

Kyle gingerly reaches out to touch Lara's back, only to startle when the cat lets out a realistic purr. "Is she a cat or a plushie?" Kyle whispers to me.

I shrug. I'm not sure, and I'm not sure it really matters.

"Lara, we've uncovered some specifics about the apocalypse," I tell her, before relaying the details about horsemen, Black Friday, and the mart. The cat shakes her head, again ready to ignore the obvious, until I add, "It's *real*, Lara. It's real, and we have to stop it."

Lara goes still.

"We need your help," I tell her. "We need to know what you know about *hell*."

"I *really* don't like talking about that stuff," Lara says. "You know that."

I get off the couch so I can sit cross-legged and be eye to eye with her. "Lara. *That stuff* is going to kill eight billion people. No more TikTok kids who do dumb shit, no more pizza joint down the corner with your favorite Hawaiian, no more YouTube, no *Friends* revival . . ." I scratch her back before adding, "No more us being best friends when we're both, you know, *dead*."

Lara lies flat on the couch. "Look, I've known for some

time that there was an apocalypse," she admits. "And—*fine!*—maybe I should've said *something*. But what would we do anyway? I figured we're better off eating pizza and watching *Friends* than crapping our pants, waiting for the end of the world."

"She's a demon, Jasper," says Kyle as she turns her back to us. "Of course she doesn't want to help."

Lara looks closely at Kyle, then me, and finally sighs.

"*Fine*. Fine! You wanna know about hell?" The cat climbs onto my lap and peers up at us. "Well, okay—the place beyond the portals isn't actually *hell*. It's a metaphysical abyss that contains humankind's darkest of thoughts, nightmares, and emotions."

I blink, hard, and try to summarize: "So, kinda like an enormous dumpster filled with humanity's psychological garbage juice?"

"Pretty much," says Lara. "But on the bright side, there's no such thing as *Satan*. So that's a win."

Kyle raises a brow. "*Sure*. That makes all the difference."

"Would you like to see the abyss? I can do, like, a Vulcan mind meld and show you some 2D visuals of it."

"Wait. You have *powers*?" I ask.

"Just close your eyes," says Lara as she places a paw each on my forehead and Kyle's. "Okay, here it is, people . . . the abyss!"

All I see is the blackness behind my eyelids.

"Lara? It's *nothing*," I tell her.

"Of course it's nothing. It's an abyss," Lara replies. "Well, it's an image of what the abyss used to look like, ages and ages ago. Now, keep your eyes shut. I'm about to show you something else. Over the past few centuries, the 'psychological garbage juice,' as you called it, has evolved into actual *life-forms*. All those human nightmares stored in the abyss . . . they've become *demons*."

A "video" of sorts emerges in my mind's eye. It's grainy and flickery, but it shows me phantasmagoric demons like the ones I've seen at the mart.

"These demons are insane, vicious, wild—well, except for the rare oddities like me." Lara pauses, and although my eyes are still closed, I reach out to pat her head. "There's more though."

"More?"

"Remember how I said that the abyss contains humankind's darkest emotions? Well, these emotions have evolved into highly intelligent spirits . . . known as *abyssals*." At those words, Lara shows us an image of humanoid silhouettes with rippling, silvery outlines—like the wraiths in my dreams. "The abyssals have supernatural powers, and they're the beings who pierced your world with portals."

Kyle gasps softly. "So, these abyssals can puncture holes in reality?"

"Oh, they can do *a lot* more. If they ever got to Earth, they'd be able to incarnate themselves inside dead bodies." Lara shows us an abyssal spirit slipping into a lifeless human corpse and bringing that form back to life. "There. *Incarnation*. The abyssals' ultimate desire."

They want to occupy human bodies?

"The abyssals want to be more than *echoes* of humanity," says Lara. She shows us an imagined scene where thousands of shimmering wraiths are sinking into dead bodies. "There are millions of abyssals, and they all want to be *real*. They want to invade your world and make it *theirs*."

I pull away from Lara. I stagger to a window to see heavy clouds block out the sun and darken the city—and my ever-present hopelessness threatens to pop out, almost like a chestburster from the *Alien* movies.

Someone reaches out to unclench my fingers, and I turn to see Kyle beside me. She simply gives me a look that says, *I know*, before leading me back to the living room.

"The abyssals want a change of scenery?" Kyle asks Lara.

Lara nods. "That's why the abyssals created those portals. Hell Portal Day was supposed to give them doorways to Earth—but as it turned out, the abyssals lacked the physical strength to actually *step through* the portals. Only the demons were able to pop through.

"The abyssals used up almost all their powers on Hell Portal Day, but refused to give up. They began examining all the portals and, eventually, found an anomalous one that was . . . soft. *Porous*. All the abyssals tried to step through this portal. But only *four of them* were strong enough to successfully cross over to Earth. These four abyssals—"

"Are the *horsemen*," Kyle and I breathe.

Who've by now surely found themselves human bodies.

Lara nods. "The 'horsemen' have a plan. They want to use their remaining powers to widen this soft portal—what we now know to be the *mart portal*—on its Earth side, while the other abyssals do the same on the abyss side. By stretching the portal on *both* ends, they'll make it so soft that *all* the other abyssals can simply waltz on through." Lara takes a deep breath. "Oh, and once the mart portal is widened, this will allow hordes and hordes of demons to flood out into Sundown City and kill tons of people."

Kyle shivers, and I *know* she's thinking the same as me: What Lara described is the thing we've been witnessing in our nightmares. Monsters killing folks to create empty shells.

"But that's just the start," Lara whispers.

"What do you mean?" I ask.

"There's millions of abyssals, so there won't be enough available corpses right away. Most of the abyssal spirits will probably end up circling the globe, looking for freshly dead bodies to slip into. You'd have no way to guess who is or isn't an abyssal. You'd never know if the old lady next door is one, until she scrapes your face off with a steel spatula. The paranoia alone—"

"Would tear the world apart," Kyle breathes.

For the longest time, Kyle and I sit in silence, holding our breaths, waiting for the dark outside to clear, as though we've never left that Baskin-Robbins. Just like that, my thoughts go back to—of all things—that fucking ice cream.

I'm not finished eating my way through the Baskin-Robbins menu.

Man, I'm not even *close* to finished with rediscovering this world.

I turn to ask Lara, "What happens when you kill an abyssal who's incarnated inside a human corpse?"

"Well, they *die*," says Lara. "Once an abyssal is fully incarnated in a physical body and the physical body dies, they die with it. It's finito for them."

"That's something, then," I reply. "Look, the horsemen seem to be the key to the apocalypse. Doomsday can't happen without them. So what if we rock up on Black Friday and just eliminate the horsemen before they can widen the portal?"

Lara mulls this over. "Well . . . the horsemen won't be easy to find. We don't know what bodies they'll be in, or even *how* to identify them. Meanwhile, all they need is a couple of minutes near the portal . . . and *bam*, they can widen it."

"How close to the portal do they need to be?" I ask.

"Well, *anywhere* in the mart could be close enough," says Lara.

"Damn. They could easily hide in the massive Black Friday crowd," says Kyle.

Kyle and Lara seem to be holding their breaths as they look to me—*me!*—to suggest what we should do.

"Uh, I . . ."

Kyle stares at me straight on, with this sort of devastating openness, as though I have any fucking clue what I'm doing. And damn, I'm not *that* guy.

"I, I—"

A cold pit swirls in my chest, but I know I have to push through it. So I wave for Kyle and Lara to step closer and try to put on an encouraging smile as I say, "We'll find a way to identify the horsemen." *Please don't ask me how.* "We can save the world. I know we can."

I reach out to place a palm on Lara's paw.

Kyle lays her hand over mine and adds, "We can do this."

"We can do this," we all echo, and then louder still. "We can do this!"

Never has a lie felt so good.

A chime fills the air, and Kyle pulls out her phone. The screen flashes red and black, over and over, until the black takes hold and shows us the red Suckerpunch logo of ⊠. A message appears below:

COME TO THE MART. NOW.

JUST YOU.

Kyle taps the screen, looking for a way to reply, but the Suckerpunch message disappears. She turns to me and says, "I should go. Maybe Suckerpunch has a way to help identify abyssals in human bodies. It's worth a shot."

"Right," I reply as she hurries to the door.

Despite the Suckerpunch request that she come alone, I'm about to offer to go with her. But then my gaze settles on her Kevlar vest and the dagger hidden inside and I think, *No, she'll be better off on her own.*

Kyle, though, lingers at the doorway to look around—at the living room, the furniture, the pictures, and finally . . . *me.* Wait, has she been here before? Were we close enough that we'd hang out in my room, work on my Ewok village, get lost in our own little world? Would my mom stick her head in to say some annoying shit like, *Hey! Who wants pizza rolls?*

Kyle points at the couch. "That's the sofa from the mart's back room, isn't it?"

"Uh, it's the couch *cover* from it. I stole it for Lara, back when she was in her Pinterest interior design phase," I reply.

"Ah! I knew something was familiar."

Right . . . That's *all* that's familiar.

Now I realize why I haven't asked Kyle about her memories of me. Without more details of my past, it's easy to pretend that she and I could've been something, anything. I sigh inwardly, and she looks like she wants to say something but doesn't know how.

In the end she shrugs. "I'll call you when it's over."

"Cool." I give her the number of my new phone (which I got after my amnesia caused me to forget my old one's unlock code). But before I can take any joy in *that*, she's already out of my place.

I turn to see Lara staring at me, paws pressed against her cheeks. "So . . . that's *Kyle.*"

I decide to change the subject. "When were you gonna tell me you had *powers*?"

Lara's paws lower, and she shrugs. "I just didn't want you to look at me like I was some kind of *monster*." When I crouch beside her, she finally mutters, "Maybe I didn't want to remember that *I* was one."

"You're not a monster," I tell her.

Her eyes meet mine, and she purrs.

A rumble in the distance. We head to a window and gaze down to see Kyle walking off to the east. But in the opposite direction, two blocks away, a large red cloud is curling above an apartment building. I peer harder, only to realize the red is a swarm of dentures gnashing at the air.

The sound of gunfire and flamethrowers can be heard.

I quickly close my window and retreat to the couch. "Things are getting wilder every day."

Lara doesn't reply.

"Hey. Can you use your powers to show me something?"

"Ooh! Sure," she chirps. "What do you want to see? My imagined version of a *Friends* revival TV show, with everyone, like, older and shit? Or maybe I could deepfake a version where everyone's a *cat*?"

"Can you show me a future? One where you, me, and Kyle manage to win?"

Lara nods. "So, a future where we exist?"

I close my eyes as she places a paw on my forehead. "No, not just exist. A future where I'm not a nobody, and where this world isn't a big series of nowheres and nothings."

"Okay," says Lara.

The blackness behind my eyes becomes an image of Kyle, Lara, and me in a park, all of us lying on grass as we seem to be cloud-watching. Lara's vision doesn't have sound, but it looks like we're laughing. Lara keeps her paw on my forehead, but I soon struggle to hold on to the image. It just . . . doesn't seem real.

Something hijacks Lara's vision, and suddenly, I see an entirely different scene: the mart on Black Friday, the portal glowing red as abyssals rush out in a parade of shimmering silhouettes, their bodies flanked by streams of demons . . .

"No!" I call out.

I try to snap out of it, but I'm locked inside this vision.

"Jasper?! Open your eyes! Come on," says Lara.

Something sharp chomps on my hand. My eyes pop open to see Lara biting my palm. She lets go, and I shudder as I realize what just happened: my Doomsday Delirium has finally showed me a hallucination. I've officially leveled up.

"Jasper! Are you okay?!" Lara calls out.

"My head," I groan.

I barely manage to lie on my side before everything melts away.

11

Survival Mode

Out of the darkness, a weird image pops up: Lara, sitting upright against a black background. Her stomach contains a rectangular screen with digits: 6:59 a.m. She's . . . an alarm clock? Lara winks as the time clicks over to 7:00 a.m. and screeches out, "Meow, meow, meow! Beep, beep, beep!" over and over.

I awake with a start. Lara is sitting beside me. She pulls her paw back from my forehead but continues making those awful sounds. She must have been projecting images of an alarm clock into my mind.

"*Please*, enough with the beeping. My head . . ."

Is pounding. I'm still on the couch, but Lara pulled a blanket over me. "How long was I unconscious?"

"Like, fifteen hours. I tried to wake you a few times, but apparently, you were extremely tired," Lara explains.

I reach for my phone and find that Kyle called three times last night. She finally left a message: **Meet me at work 2morrow. Got BIG NEWS.**

Out in the street, I make my way through the roadblocks, traffic, and crowds as I hurry to work. *What did Kyle find out?* That thought keeps looping—but then I pass a hair salon whose entrance is cordoned off by hazard tape.

Blood is running out of the entry. Not a lot but enough that it's noticeable. Yet people just walk on by like it's no big deal, just another day in paradise. And all I can think of is that the nearest portal is two streets away. Monsters are not supposed to be able to get so far from a VC quarantine.

I notice the kid in the green hoodie from yesterday.

He's standing near the blood, shivering faintly. He pulls out his phone and, clearly, is trying to open his VC app. "Come on, come on," he mutters. He tiptoes closer to the battle scene, until his phone chimes with points.

"*Hey!*" I yell out.

Hoodie Kid recognizes me and darts off down the street. But he doesn't get far. He slips on a McDonald's wrapper, trips to the ground, and his phone lands a couple of steps away. He gets up quickly, but not before I grab the phone.

"Hey! That's mine!" he yells. He tries to grab back the phone, but I hold my arm up and all he can do is hop around. "Give it!"

I shake my head. "I've had enough of you. I'm deleting your VC app."

"Dude, I need my points!"

"Geez! Is this actually fun for you?"

The boy halts, pulls down his hood to glare. "Fun? I use points to buy food, dipshit. You think I like doing *this*?" he asks, waving his hand at not just the bloodied salon, but *everything*.

I notice dirt stains on his skin. His clothes have rips.

"Where are your parents, kid?" I clam up as soon as the question is out of my mouth.

"I'm not a kid," he mutters with an all-too-familiar hardness. And I think I finally understand Penelope and Dean's inside joke about F-16s: Maybe every young person has been jettisoned into adulthood. The F-16s are simply the ones getting hazard pay.

"I—"

Hoodie Boy lunges to jab a finger in the soft part of my stomach. I double over, and he grabs his phone back and starts running. But before he can get far, I yell out after him, "*Hey!* Wait. You . . . want my points? I can transfer them to you."

After Kyle's point-grabbing in the MDA, we split the extra points between us, which gave me 3,400 VC.

The boy stops to face me, shifts about warily. "Sure." He holds out his phone but doesn't get too close.

I open my VC app and press *TRANSFER*. I let my device scan for his, and then click another button to send him my points.

He lowers his gaze and shrugs. "Um. Thanks."

He's about to cross the street, but freezes when a man, a woman, and a little boy stroll down the opposite sidewalk, holding hands. Hoodie Boy's shoulders sag, and I want to tell him he's not alone. But then the family skips cheerily over a blood puddle, and Hoodie Boy scowls.

"Sometimes I wanna scream my head off, just to see if that would change anything," he mumbles. "But *nothing* ever changes."

"I refuse to believe that nothing can—"

Hoodie Boy starts to walk off, and I know there's nothing I could say to change this moment. And maybe I have no fucking right to tell him what to do. So I take in a deep breath . . . and *scream* like a maniac. The family fun troop stops, startled. Hoodie Boy freezes too, until he turns to face me and howls just as loud, and the family darts away as if we're demons.

The kid and I bowl over, cackling, until a patroller heads our way and we dart in opposite directions. But before we do, we share a nod.

I get to the mart only to find it's not yet open. I step into the back room as Gully starts rounding up all the clerks for a morning meeting. I have no choice but to bide my time until I can catch up with Kyle.

Gully is manic today. He sounds super twitchy, like his voice is high up in his chest. He reminds us that Black Friday is two days away and that we need to do everything possible to win the Here For You head office's Black Friday cash prize. Which is when he lays on the kicker: "To maximize our profits on the big day, I'll be opening the store at *midnight*. Which means we'll be staying open for twenty-four straight hours!"

The horsemen could strike at any time during that twenty-four-hour window.

My gaze shifts to the people around me—who all seem to be in various states of disbelief that our Black Friday just *doubled*—and I wonder if one of them could be a horseman.

I use my phone under a table to type a message to Lara: **How can I tell if someone's a horseman?**

Although Lara has no fingers, I've enabled voice commands on all devices at home. She replies swiftly: **Hard to tell. Could be anyone, honestly.**

I text her back: **There must be clues? Body odor? Strange shadows? Gimme something.**

Her reply: **The horsemen will have blended in by now. They have access to knowledge about this world. So, yeah, there's no real tip-offs that I know.**

"Great . . . ," I mumble.

Gully catches me drifting off and slams a meaty palm on the table in front of me. "Jasper! Do you want me to put you on the midnight shift for Black Friday?"

Actually, that would be ideal. I'd have the perfect cover to be here from the start.

"Uh . . . ," I begin.

Gully rolls his eyes. "Bah, it's better you take the day shift. You're *hopeless*. I need all the best hands at the start."

As he walks away, I know I need to poke the bear: "Um. Is it even legal for us to be working at midnight?"

Gully stops in his tracks. Turns around to glare. "Okay, dude. For that insubordination, you get the midnight shift."

And just like that, I've booked a front-row ticket for the biggest show in town.

The minute the morning meeting is over, I hurry out into the store's center—just in time to catch sight of Kyle. Our eyes meet, and I'm about to head over to her, until Gully barks at me to get over behind checkout one. Once I'm there, Gully pokes my shoulder and says with a smirk, "*Stay!*"—as if I'm some sort of Labrador—and I find myself powerless to fight his retail overlord energy.

Soon shoppers are streaming in, and Kyle has disappeared into Vanguard duty. Gully is wandering about, mouthing commands like *Smile!* and *Be friendly!* as though we're in a charm school for the budget-conscious. All I can do is hope that somehow time passes more quickly than it usually does.

Eventually, at midday, Gully tires of lording over us and leaves work early. And as soon as I see him bolt, I throw up a REGISTER CLOSED sign and race off to look for Kyle. I find her, finally, near the door to the back room. She waves for me to follow, and we end up in the moldy storeroom from yesterday.

Sealed away from the world, she greets me, "Hey."

"Hey. Sorry I didn't answer your calls yesterday. I passed out from . . . well . . . everything. Whatever. Tell me what happened with Suckerpunch."

"So much to discuss," she says. "So, last night, I got here just before closing time. I thought I'd get to meet a Suckerpunch person in the flesh, but instead, I got another message on my phone. It said to meet in the mart's photo booth."

My phone chimes.

Lara has sent me a message: **Any updates?**

"Hold on," I tell Kyle as I get Lara on a video call.

"Hey, guys," Lara says as her face appears on-screen.

"I've got news to share," Kyle tells us, before she explains that Suckerpunch hijacked the preview screen inside the photo booth and turned it into a live chat feed. "There was this hacker dude—his face and voice digitally distorted—and he asked me what I wanted. So I told him what we'd learned, you know, about the apocalypse."

"And?" I ask.

"And it turns out Suckerpunch has been aware of rumors that Doomies' apocalypse visions might be real. But when I asked him for help, the hacker dude just told me something totally crazy." Kyle takes in a deep breath before adding, "According to him, VC knows how to *close* portals."

My eyes widen, and she nods.

"*Yeah*, you heard me right."

"Whoa . . . ," Lara gasps. "So, what's the secret?"

"Suckerpunch doesn't know exactly," says Kyle. "But the hacker was adamant that VC's head honchos are hiding this knowledge."

Lara leans in so close to her phone screen that all I see is her nose. "If we knew the secret to closing portals, we could just close the mart portal *before* Black Friday." She leans back, her head in her paws. "The abyssals haven't got enough remaining power to create new portals. Heck, they don't even know *why* the mart portal is porous. So if we get rid of that soft portal, they'd have no way to invade!"

That sounds too good to be true. "But all this depends on VC actually having this 'secret.' And us getting it."

Kyle purses her lips. "Yeah, that's the tricky bit." She pulls out her phone and shows me a photo of the VC asylum—the one I pass each day—and points out a structure just to its right. "This other building is a high-security VC facility. CCTV cameras everywhere. Top-level clearance just to get in." She exhales as she lowers the phone. "It's totally inaccessible for trainees like me."

"You think the info is in that facility?" I ask.

"According to Suckerpunch, it is. The secret is kept on a file inside an air-gapped computer deep in there," says Kyle.

"Air-gapped?" Lara asks.

"It's a device *not* connected to any network or internet. It's unhackable," says Kyle. "Which is why Suckerpunch needs our help."

"What do you mean?" Lara asks.

My phone screen fritzes as Lara's video signal drops out, but I'm too distracted to call her back. "Our help?" I ask.

Kyle nods. "Suckerpunch says it could hack the computer if someone—*us*—were to go inside that building and manually connect the computer to the internet."

"What did you tell them?"

"I said it was not gonna be easy," she replies. "Which was an understatement. There's no way we can get into that building."

Kyle puts away her phone, and I'm about to ask what we should do next, until she beats me to the punch: "So . . . what now?" And once again, she's looking at me as though *I'm* the one who has all our answers.

"I don't know." I shake my head. "Look. Yesterday, when you asked me what we should do next, I know I said that we can do this. But, seriously . . . I had no damn clue." I gaze off into the shadows. "I keep thinking that something will click, but if I'm being honest, I think I'm just trying to forget the hopelessness inside me." When I finally meet her gaze, her calm unnerves me. "Kyle, the end of the world is coming, and really, all I've got to offer is, like, a bumper sticker that reads *YOU GOT THIS*."

Kyle studies me and then shrugs. "Dude, I've spent such a long time trying not to do or feel anything. Like I've been stuck in some bomb shelter, waiting for the fallout to clear. But *you* reminded me that we can *act*. We can do something—"

"I had my first *waking* vision last night."

Her eyes widen.

"The future is literally driving me crazy." When Kyle goes silent, I roll my shoulders and add, "You know, this is where you're supposed to say: *No, Jasper, you're not going crazy.*"

"So what if you're crazy?" Kyle says after a long beat. "The whole world's a mess of shards held together by Krazy Glue."

She gets up and leads me to the doorway between the back room and the aisles. We glimpse people rushing to aisle five for a flash sale on SpongeBob SquarePants toilet paper. I spot a few of our regulars who practically live here, like this pregnant woman who seems to think that the garden section will eventually be her nursery.

"*This* is way crazier than you'll ever be," she says.

We're so close to one another, her hair brushing against my neck.

"Do you feel crazy too?" I ask, almost a whisper.

Kyle grabs my hand and leads me back toward a shadowy corner of the back room, turning briefly on the way to say, "Let me show you *my* crazy."

Kyle guides me to a small, locked door I've never noticed before. She fishes out a key, checks we're alone, then unlocks the door to reveal a hidden stairwell. "Come on," she whispers as she guides me in and shuts the door behind us.

A faint light is coming from below. Kyle and I head down

a dozen steps to a tiny basement. The walls are lined with Christmas trees in all shapes and sizes, each decked out in tinsel, lights, ornaments, and glitter stars. The ground is covered in Styrofoam beads that mimic snow.

I chuckle. "What the . . . You did this?"

Kyle sits on a box wrapped in red-and-green paper. I settle in next to her.

"Last month, I discovered that Marco stored boxes of unused Christmas stuff here. So . . . I thought I'd open everything and arrange it nicely, like my parents did when I was little."

"Yeah?"

"My parents are from Taiwan. They always said that they came to America so I could be anything and have *everything*. Immigrant Parenting 101." She fluffs a tree. "Christmas at our place was like that on steroids. We had presents everywhere. Which I fucking hated, because I somehow knew we couldn't afford so much stuff. I'd always try to tell them, 'I don't even *want* everything.' But then, of course, after Hell Portal Day . . ."

Everything isn't even a possibility anymore.

When she goes silent, I just nod. "Yeah."

Kyle rolls her shoulders, gazing at a few boxes. "But when I sensed that this apocalypse could be real, I realized maybe I *do* want *everything* . . . or at least the dumb promise of everything." She gestures around us. "I know, this looks totally crazy—"

"I dunno. Maybe you need to go a little crazy sometimes

to stay a little *sane*."

She breaks into a big grin and whispers, "Then let's go a little crazy." She opens a music app and hits play on a song—Belinda Carlisle's "Heaven Is a Place on Earth."

Kyle starts dancing, and suddenly we're moving in time together, our arms brushing against trees, her hair caught tangling in curtains of tinsel. There's not a lot of space. I trip on the beads, and we end up sprawled on our backs, where we start making snow angels in the Styrofoam and laughing so hard it hurts.

Kyle blasts the music louder, and I wonder if anyone upstairs can hear us. Soon I realize I don't care if they do.

Our arms swing around making angel wings until our hands connect, *lock*, and—

This. Feels. Like. *Everything*.

I'm about to say something stupid, but the song comes to an end, and abruptly we're back in the real world, with our real problems. I take a deep breath and say instead, "Tell Suckerpunch we'll do it."

She raises a brow, but I add, "We'll find a way."

We'll probably get it wrong, but it's not like there's anyone else trying to right this shit anyway.

Kyle notices then that we're holding hands, and her expression clouds. She gently pulls away from me and turns to the side to grab her phone, and says, "Replying to Suckerpunch now." As she does, Kyle keeps her back to me, and I want to ask, *What's wrong? What'd I do?*

But then she says, "Okay. Message sent."

A burst of static emerges from her VC comm device, and she answers, "Kuan here."

A man's voice replies to her: "McCall here. I'm ready to take over the shift."

"Roger. I'm coming out for the handover."

Kyle turns off her comm and faces me. She's got this weird all-business look in her eyes. "My shift's over," she says, "but I'm gonna go home and wait for Suckerpunch to reply. I'll also brainstorm ideas on how to get into that building."

"Later, then," I tell her.

"Later," she repeats, gaze falling to the Styrofoam beads.

I really want to ask what's wrong, but she's already heading up to the back room two steps at a time. By the time I get to the top, all I see is her back as she leaves through the rear exit.

Standing in the shadows of Christmas, nothing makes sense.

12

Eye on You

When I return to the main floor, a few clerks are gathered in the space between the aisles and the back wall. They're frozen in place. It looks like one of those viral mannequin challenges. Gully must be trying to get our store some social media attention. Up ahead, Marco is standing just beyond aisle eleven, frozen but waving for me to come over and join in.

"*Really?*" I mutter as I move closer, until I realize he's actually waving me away and mouthing, *Get help*. Throughout the store, the customers are like statues, freeze-framed mid-scream or while reaching for expired cereal. Marco's the only person faking it.

Via a security mirror on the ceiling, I see a humanoid creature stomping its way over from aisle eleven. The beast notices Marco, growls, then covers him in a blue flash of light. Suddenly Marco is no longer pretending, but truly frozen. . . .

Even just catching a distant glimpse of that blue light

makes my limbs feel stiff. Using the security mirror by the front of the mart, I see more of the creature: It's six feet tall, covered in purple scales like on a dragon fruit. It has only one *enormous* shimmery blue eye. I see a knife slash of a mouth.

A rat scurries out from under an aisle and squeaks. The demon turns toward the sound, then shoots a blue beam to freeze it before trundling over to squish it for fun.

Should I run? Should I hide? No time. All I can do is focus my eyes on a fixed spot and pretend to be frozen too.

The creature walks right past me, and I hold my breath and keep as still as I can. Its fleshy dragon-fruit scales flutter to reveal serpent tongues hidden below. It pauses to scan the store.

The beast spots the store's CCTV cameras. It seems to mistake these for animals, and it shoots out blue beams to fry the cams. Somehow it must have fried the front sliding doors too. No new shoppers are entering the store.

I slowly pull out my phone to use the VC app to summon help, but my battery is dead. My only chance is to get to the back room to push the *EMERGENCY* VC button.

When the monster turns the corner and heads up aisle ten, I make my move, creeping around in the opposite direction. But only a dozen steps in, I glimpse aisle seven to see a curly-haired little girl crouching there. She's shaking, crying, clutching a teddy bear. I mime for her to shush as I slip over to help her, but she runs over and throws herself into my arms. And bumps a nearby basket.

My gaze shoots to a ceiling-mounted security mirror, and I see the monster turn in our direction.

Quickly, I lower the girl and point at the door to the back room. She shakes her head, but I mouth, *Go!* She hesitates a beat, but then does as I ask. To buy her time, I kick over the sunglasses rack and the cheap shades scatter everywhere.

The monster whirls, and I dart toward the back room, but before I can even leave aisle seven, the demon appears in front of me. Instantly I squeeze my eyes shut and yell out in my head, *Don't look at the light!* I reach blindly for something, *anything*, to use as a weapon, and end up grabbing a spray can from a nearby shelf. I hurl it as hard as I can at the monster.

No surprise, I miss.

I hear the can roll and *clang* off into the distance.

I'm about to just make a run for it, when I realize that the beast's blue light hasn't flared.

I dare to open my eyes, and lo and behold, the demon is on its hands and knees in front of me. It's holding the spray can in its mouth. It lets out a low but somehow *playful* growl before dropping the can at my feet. It scampers so close I can smell it—rotting meat and sweat. Its scales flutter as it butts its head against my knee.

It yips. Seriously, it *yips*.

Does it want to . . . *play*? I reach down for the spray can, try not to focus on the monster slobber, and toss it to the far end of the aisle.

The monster bounds away and pounces on the can.

Moments later, it drops the can at my feet again. Squeals.

Fuck me, this demon has the temperament of the typical family dog.

I pick up the can and toss it toward the farthest checkout. The beast chases it, and I'm about to race for the back room until I remember there's also an *EMERGENCY* button in aisle nine itself.

I slip through the damaged gate. Aaron and his fellow guard are frozen beside the portal, but I know I can't help them right now. Instead, I rush to a wall panel and slam the *EMERGENCY* button.

Backup should arrive in a few minutes.

But then the demon scurries into aisle nine, chirps, and plops a new item at my feet. Not the spray can, but a prosthetic *hand*. Where the fuck did it get that? It had to have taken it off a shopper. I shiver as I stare at teeth marks.

Oh God . . .

The monster senses my hesitation and stands. Those scales flutter about faster and faster, and the air fills with a hissing. I take a step back, but it moves closer.

A rattle echoes on the opposite end of the aisle.

I see Kyle unlock the other gate. She's holding a chunky rifle and points her weapon at the demon's back. Her only armor is her Kevlar vest and what looks like a pair of ski goggles.

"*Kyle!*" I hiss. "No!"

The beast turns and blasts Kyle with blue light. I barely have time to shield my face. But when the glow fades, I see Kyle smirk, shake her head, and shoot.

A fleshy *pop* fills the air. The demon shrieks, grabs at its eye, and slumps against the far edge of the quarantine zone. Kyle stalks over, firing a dozen more shots along the way. The whites of its eye turn into a goopy mush, then a strawberry pink as blood mingles. The beast sinks to its knees, gasping.

Kyle tries to keep firing, but her weapon jams.

"Shit," she hisses as she changes a cartridge.

The creature lunges blindly at her, an arm outstretched like a bloody bayonet. I rush over, push the beast to the side, and it jerks around to try to swing at me.

Razor-sharp nails graze my forearm. I cry out.

"Jasper!" Kyle yells.

I stagger back as Kyle gets her gun unjammed and manages to shoot the beast in its ruined eye—again and again and again. It's more than dead by the time she finally drops her weapon and rushes over to my side. I try to tell her I'm fine, but tears stream down her face as she holds on to me tightly.

"I'm . . . I'm okay," I tell her. "It's just a scratch."

"You . . . that thing . . . It almost killed you," she mutters, shaking away the thought.

In the corner of my eye, I see the portal ripple. It warbles and quivers, as though it's got an upset stomach, until without warning, the center of it sprouts a large black tendril that swirls around us like a lasso. And before we can even scream, the tendril yanks us both in.

PART
TWO

The Abyss

The darkness is a velvet thing that twists and stretches around me, smothering my screams, threatening to crush me, until suddenly, it spits me out. I land, hard, on solid ground but don't feel pain. I get to my knees, try to suck in a breath but taste nothing, feel nothing. Are my eyes even open? *Are we . . . in the abyss?*

"Kyle!"

"I'm here."

My eyes adjust. She's kneeling beside me; our hands connect, but I can't feel her touch. She says what I'm thinking: "This place feels like nothing. Like I'm dreaming."

Or maybe more accurately—*nightmaring.*

The wasteland around us is lit by faint lights scattered in the distance. The ground is made of glittering black crags and broken up by puddles in all sorts of dark colors.

But as strange as it all looks, the landscape somehow seems *familiar*—like I've been here before, with every sleepless night, every disappointment, every unkind thought about myself and others, every feeling I've tried to ignore, every sense that the world is dissolving around me, every fear that I'm just not enough. Somehow, this feels less like a descent into alien territory and more like a *homecoming*.

Kyle stares numbly around us, then sinks to a crouch.

"You feel it too?" I whisper.

Kyle blinks once, twice, then spots something ahead. "Jasper! Look!"

I follow her gaze. Two dozen yards away there's a flickering circle of gray light—and I think it's our mart portal. It *has* to be.

We get up and hurry in that direction, holding on to one another's hand, until I trip on a crag. I tumble to the ground, barely shielding my head from cracking against a rock. And yet somehow, it doesn't hurt.

Instead, I'm struck by a weird thought: *I could disappear and no one would notice.* I'm about to say those words out loud, but then my gaze settles on a dark blue puddle I'm touching. I see the water trembling.

I stagger backward and wipe my hand on my pant leg. My head clears, and I whisper, "The liquid . . . It's like it contained a thought—" I see Kyle kneeling motionlessly nearby. "Kyle? You okay?" And when I get no response, I yell out, "Kyle?"

"Stop asking if I'm okay," Kyle mutters.

"I'm just—"

Kyle is knee-deep in a crescent-shaped puddle of maroon

water. I head over to the puddle edge and tell her to get up. But she turns and snaps, "Stop trying to help me."

I open my mouth, but she doesn't let me speak.

"Stop telling me things will be okay—like you actually even give a shit!"

"Kyle. The liquid—" I try to get her out of the water, but when I reach for her arm, she shoves me away, and the water, or whatever it is, splashes my neck. Instantly, I feel something—not a thought, but a twisting inside my chest. "*Hey!* We don't have time for this shit! Stop lashing out at me!" I grab her by the shoulders.

Kyle tries to wrestle out of my grip, but I refuse to let go, and we end up rolling into a shallow body of gray water. This liquid soaks the side of my shirt, and my anger is instantly replaced by a deep desire to just stop *trying*.

Kyle turns away. She won't look at me, but her neck and arms are gray with droplets. I try to reach her, but she stutters, "It's pointless . . . I . . . I'm always gonna keep messing things up." She shifts farther away from me.

"Kyle," I call out.

Somehow, I find the strength to fight that desire to give up. I struggle to my feet. I don't know how I'm doing this. But maybe hopelessness is a drug and I'm a junkie with a helluva tolerance for it.

Shakily, I guide us both to dry ground, then wrap my arms around her. "Hey, hey, hey . . . listen to me. It's the *water*. I think all the pools have thoughts or emotions."

She tries to speak, but I just hold on tighter. When I finally pull away, I take off my work vest and use it to wipe my arms and hands, then her face and arms. "It's not us."

Abruptly, Kyle catches sight of something and freezes. I follow her gaze a dozen yards to the right, where motion emerges from behind a boulder. Kyle and I drop low just as a demon steps into view. It's a humanoid made of what appears to be pink cake frosting. Oversized sprinkles are stuck all over its body. It has candles wedged in its eye sockets; the beast seems to be trying to pull out those candles—or, maybe, push them deeper in. It's hard to tell.

Although the creature doesn't have eyes, it swivels its head about, as though to scan the place. And I know we need to hide. I catch sight of a shallow crater to our right, and mouth to Kyle, *There!* Together, we quietly slip into the crater and drop just below the surface level. Unfortunately, my side touches a puddle that ripples in dark rainbow colors.

This puddle takes my mind . . . somewhere else.

One moment I'm in the abyss, the next I'm standing inside what seems like a medical ward. I'm surrounded by doctors, nurses, armed guards, and patients in thin white gowns. The patients are all strapped to beds. Is this a VC asylum? I try to look around but can't.

I think I'm stuck in someone else's point of view. A *memory.*

I catch sight of my reflection in a glass door. Somehow, I'm a tall guy in a VC uniform. A guard. Behind me in the same reflection, a young male patient is trying to sneak away. Must be a Doomie. In the memory, I turn around to lunge at the patient and punch him in the chest.

The Doomie sprawls on the floor.

I grab the young Doomie by his hair and drag him in the direction of a nurse. "Keep them in check," I bark.

With a gasp, I snap out of the memory and shift away from the puddle. Kyle also shivers, and I sense she too witnessed that scene. However, neither of us speak as we peer above the crater to see that the cake-frosting demon has gone.

We get to our feet and try to go back to the portal. But Kyle slips on a loose rock and falls into a trench of rainbow water.

"Shit! Kyle!!!" I drop to my knees, ready to reach in after her.

The light shifts.

Something emerges to my left. A silhouette that twists and buckles in the air. *It's an . . . abyssal!* I stumble backward, and my movement tugs the creature toward me, like a thin plastic bag into a breeze. I freeze as it hovers a dozen steps away, spreads out shifting arms, and *speaks.* Not with words, but somehow with the vibrations of the abyss air itself.

You! You, you, you! Come closer, it says tonelessly.

"Get away from me!" I hiss.

I retreat another step. But it just gets even closer. I might as well be back in that gray puddle, for a sinking feeling soaks through me and makes me think, *What's the point in trying to fight? Why am I bothering to even try anything?*

But then, out of the corner of my eye, I see something. The maroon puddle from earlier. It's only two steps away. I use all my remaining strength to step into this liquid, and instantly, my despair morphs into rage. Suddenly I'm ready to punch anyone in my way, over and over, till my knuckles match the puddle. But since I can't touch the abyssal, I simply open my mouth and go fucking apeshit. *"Get away from me!"* I roar, again and again. *"I'm not afraid of you!"*

The abyssal might as well be a birthday candle, blown out by the wish of my words.

I rush over to the trench that Kyle fell into, and I reach in to try to grab her hand.

But then the water decides to show me a memory. I'm standing in my folks' living room. In a window, my reflection shows *Kyle*. I'm . . . in one of *her* recollections, seeing through her eyes.

She says sharply in the scene, "I can't do this anymore with you." And she turns around to face *me*.

In the memory, I call out, "Kyle. You can't want—"

Kyle steps backward and says, "You know what I really want? I want to stop going around in circles with you."

Don't get stuck in this memory! I tell myself abruptly. *Get out! Hurry! Quick!*

Shuddering, I pull myself free and lift Kyle out of the water and onto the rocky ground. She coughs, chokes, but gets to her feet, and soon, we race over to the portal and throw ourselves back through the circle of light.

Blood Buggy

We stagger out of the portal, flee aisle nine, and sprawl out in the two-for-one section. The lights are flickering, and CCTV cams are smoldering. Most of the shoppers and staff are still frozen—including the guards—though a few people are slowly regaining movement. To our right, a shopper unfreezes to scream, only to realize there's nothing terrifying in front of her anymore. "What happened? Wasn't there a *demon*?"

The other folks start to stir.

Lieutenant Shiner stumbles over, his eyes bloodshot from being frozen. He blinks and takes in the dead monster in aisle nine, then composes himself to call out, "*Attention.* The beast has been defeated. No need to fear, people."

Shoppers seem to think the lieutenant slew the beast, and they start clapping like he just won an Olympic gold.

I ignore him and help Kyle off the ground. Surprisingly, our clothes are dry. She steadies herself but doesn't meet my gaze. Somehow I *know* she knows what I saw in the memory pool. The recollection of hers, where the two of us . . .

Us . . . ! There's an *us* in my past.

"Kyle—"

We're still holding hands, and I suddenly gaze at the ground to see the shapes we cast. The connected silhouettes of two kids made of shadow. But before I can focus back on Kyle, a shopper taps me on my shoulder, and says, "Orthotics?" And just like that, Kyle pulls away from me as the stranger asks more loudly, "Dude, where's orthotics?"

"Aisle ten," I tell him.

I'm about to go after Kyle, but the back room doors burst open to let in six Vanguardians—the backup I summoned with the *EMERGENCY* button. These guys march over to the aisle nine quarantine, and Shiner gives them orders to "lock down the store."

Half the soldiers are tasked with escorting shoppers outside, while the others begin cleaning aisle nine and repairing its gate. Shiner tells Kyle to help, but before she goes off, her gaze flutters to meet mine, and for the life of me, I can't read her expression.

Shiner pulls out his walkie-talkie and calls out, "Attention, staff! Proceed to the break room. *Now*." He must have logged his comms into the PA. His voice booms through all the speakers. He catches sight of me and lowers his walkie. Studies me for a beat. Does he somehow know that I went through the portal? How could he? But then one of the last few lingering shoppers pushes a cart packed with toilet paper like a mobile iceberg in between Shiner and me. He roars at her to leave, and I use the distraction to slip away.

Moments later I'm in the break room, where all the clerks mill about as we wait for the portal quarantine to be repaired. Through the doorway, distant figures can be seen on the other side of the back room: Shiner debriefing Kyle, Aaron, and the other portal guard.

But before long, my attention goes to the Kyle memory that I glimpsed, and I cannot resist the urge to search my brain for *my own* recollection of that time. Yet as always, my amnesia fights back. My head zings, sharper than ever, until my vision blackens.

Next thing I know, I'm sitting on the floor and a Vanguard nurse in white is telling me, "Easy. You must be in shock. Eat this." She hands me a juice box and a sandwich, and then examines the scratches on my arm that were caused by the eye monster.

Things are a blur as I finish my sandwich (turkey and cheese—not bad) and the nurse fixes up my arm with disinfectant and bandages. Soon she's handing me a medical certificate. "Take the day off, kid," she tells me, giving me two thousand VC points for my "occupational incident."

I shuffle over to the door that leads to the main store. I see a new aisle nine gate and a new churning mass of shoppers, as though nothing ever happened. But then I look behind me to see Kyle sitting in the shadows of a vending machine, her knees pulled up to her chest.

I head over, sit beside her.

"You . . . okay?" I ask.

All my other questions fall to the wayside, because right now, all I want to do is put my arms around her and tell her we're safe, we're okay.

Kyle meets my gaze, then notices my bandages and shudders. "Yeah. You?" she whispers.

"Now? Yeah—"

Her phone chimes. Its screen glows with the Suckerpunch logo. Kyle holds it between us just as a message appears: **ARE YOU SERIOUS ABOUT UNCOVERING THE PORTAL-CLOSING SECRET?**

Kyle and I swap a look, then nod at one another, before she types a response: **Yes.**

The phone flickers.

OKAY. THEN YOU HAVE TO HURRY.

HEAD TO THE ALLEY BEHIND THE STORE. NOW.

Kyle and I dart out to the alley, positioning ourselves in the CCTV blind spot. Her phone chimes again, and this time the screen shows a coppery, pixelated face on a video chat.

"Jasper?" says a distorted voice. "Long time no see."

I blink. *We know each other?*

"No time to talk. I have a way for you to get to the VC facility . . . undetected. The CCTV cameras in the city are currently undergoing a security update. Street cams are getting reset one by one, which is creating shifting blind spots that you can use to get close to the VC building. But you have to follow my lead—exactly."

"Okay," says Kyle, looking at me as if to confirm we're not crazy for agreeing.

"What do we need to do?" I ask.

"In ten seconds, you need to leave the alley and cross to the opposite street," he tells us.

We count down and then dart out, and soon the Suckerpunch guy is giving us second-by-second directions through the city. Kyle holds the phone close between us, so we both can hear him, and every so often he yells, "Faster! You need to stay within the blind spots!"

To clear the way, Kyle tells random pedestrians, "Outta the way! VC business!" And when that doesn't work fast enough, I shout, "Fifty percent off all clothing at the Here For You mart! Black Friday starts early, people!"

That gets feet charging.

On and on we go, and belatedly I realize the sky is really dark for this time of day. I smell smoke everywhere.

"Ash," Kyle whispers.

There must be a brimstone situation somewhere ahead. The hacker guy says, "There were five brimstone events today."

Things are heating up as we get closer to the end of times. . . .

Eventually, hacker guy tells us, "And here you are."

But we're not at the VC building; we're a dozen feet away from a burrito joint and a large black van with a VC logo.

Kyle startles and says, "That's a Vanguard scrubber van."

"Because of all those brimstone events citywide, VC has retasked all available workers—including scrubbers—to help clean up ash," says the hacker. "This van is empty. You have twenty seconds to get inside it before your blind spot evaporates."

"*Wait! What?* You want us to steal a VC van?" Kyle hisses.

"No time to explain. You've got fifteen seconds to get behind those tinted windows and avoid being seen on CCTV."

"Shit, shit, shit," I mutter, looking around. Over in the burrito joint, two men in overalls—the scrubbers out of their hazmat suits—are ordering at the counter. They'll be done in seconds.

Kyle tries opening the van's front doors. They're locked. Crap. We circle around to the back of the van, then notice that the rear doors have jammed on a plastic cord.

We yank open these doors, scurry inside, and shut them behind us, fast as we can. Safe inside the van, we stumble into the front. Kyle dives into the driver's side, and I take the passenger seat. We're hidden behind heavily tinted glass, but—

"What now?" I ask.

Kyle stares behind us at the hazmat suits in the van, then at the vehicle dashboard. "This is our way in?" she asks the hacker. "Disguised as scrubbers?"

The guy doesn't answer. He just says: "Make sure to

cover the inner camera before you start the engine." Kyle grabs a roll of duct tape from the ground, tears off a strip, and covers a lens on the dashboard. "Now go! Before those VC assholes come back for their van."

Through the side window, I see the scrubbers heading our way. "Go!" I hiss.

Kyle turns a key still in the ignition. The scrubbers yell out when they hear the engine, but before they can even take a step, Kyle throws us into drive and peels away.

"You're outside the blind spots," says the hacker dude.

"We're outside *everything*," I whisper.

The law. The rules. Maybe even our minds. . . .

15

Franklin and Chen

Swerving, honking, and banking briefly onto an empty patch of sidewalk, Kyle manages to get us ahead of the traffic and away from the scrubbers. But then, a dozen yards ahead, our path is shuttered by a series of VC roadblocks.

I call out, "Hacker dude! We need help—"

But Kyle doesn't wait. She lays on the horn, sending nearby workers scurrying, and blasts *through* the roadblocks and over those rubber "slow down!" bumps. It creates a loud, rapid thudding like the drumroll for the announcement of *Ladies and gentlemen! Here come the winners of the Flying by the Seat of Their Pants award!*

All I can do is stare at Kyle—the only thing actually in focus—as she begins laughing, nervously at first, and then in a holler. I can't help joining in, laughing like our lives depend on it.

We turn a corner to follow the barbwire perimeter that surrounds the asylum and the VC high-security facility. We pull up to a large, metal boom gate and hush like everything only just got serious.

"Any advice?" Kyle asks the Suckerpunch hacker.

"Nope," he replies.

"Well, I'm glad we didn't do anything impulsive," I mutter, and my heart races again as a soldier leaves a security booth to head over. "Shit. Get in a scrubber suit!" I tell Kyle, climbing into the rear of the van to grab one. Kyle joins me, our hands fumbling wildly.

The soldier knocks on the van side. "Roll down the window."

"One second!" I call out as we each put on a scrubber helmet with an opaque black visor, then scramble back to our seats.

"Window down. *Now.*"

Kyle rolls down her window as I adjust my helmet and hope it's on right. Kyle's name tag reads *CHEN R.*, mine *FRANKLIN B.*

"Good day, sir," says Kyle, to a tall middle-aged guy in a gray VC uniform. "We need to get into the facility."

"Your vehicle isn't cleared to enter."

"We've been on back-to-back cleaning jobs, and we need to use an incinerator ASAP," says Kyle, looking back over her shoulder. "Who knows what the toxic goo in the back is gonna turn into. We'll be in and out in a few minutes."

The man's beady eyes don't blink. "You're not on the list."

Kyle wavers, so I lean over to say, "Buddy, please."

"Don't *buddy* me. It's not my job to make yours easier."

"Seriously?" I might as well have lingering maroon droplets on me. "Y'know what isn't in *our* job description? Brimstone cleanup. We were all set to dump our biowaste at an incinerator, until we got ordered to help city cleaners handle all this brimstone. We've literally been on the go all day."

He tries to speak, but I power on.

"Dude, I accidentally sucked a pinkie finger into one of my suit pouches, and it's rattling like candy! Can you just be a damn human being for a minute and let us use your fucking incinerator?"

The man grits his jaw, and I hold my breath.

Did I go too far?

"Please . . . *sir*," I add.

"Fine," the soldier mutters, before stepping aside and waving at a colleague to raise the boom gate. "Drive into the facility's parking garage. There's an incinerator at the far left of the garage interior. I'll expect you back out in *five* minutes."

"Thank you!" Kyle replies, before driving us toward the garage.

"Here goes nothing," I whisper as we enter a concrete dungeon.

A rolling door closes behind us with a thud.

A minute later, Kyle rolls the van into the farthest spot from the front gate and turns off the ignition. My pulse is hammering away in my ears. We've got five minutes before that soldier checks on us. Maybe less before the real Franklin and Chen report this van missing.

"Wow, you're in," says the Suckerpunch guy as Kyle pulls her phone out of a suit pocket. "I've gotta hang up so I can add the finishing touches to my remote hack for the VC computer. If you're not captured in the next few minutes, call me back. 'Kay?"

Kyle drums her palms nervously on the dashboard. "We'll need to get inside and find our way to the data archive. So we'll need a distraction." She peers at the rear of the vehicle, where walls are covered in drawers and fold-up workstations. "Maybe there's something here."

Kyle climbs into the back. I follow, careful to avoid the heavy black bags that surely contain human remains from the scrubbers' earlier shifts.

We start going through drawers, and I ask, "What are we even looking for?"

"This," says Kyle, as she crouches in front of a large box that contains a clear bag. A bag that holds a bowling ball–sized chunk of *brimstone*. (Which must have landed in something super soft to avoid powderizing.)

"Hot damn," I hiss. "That giant thing oughta be in the Smithsonian."

Kyle takes off her stained scrubber suit, then grabs two brand-new ones from a drawer. She eyes the plastic pouches attached to the suit exteriors, then says, "These pouches fill up with vacuumed blood and dirt. . . . I think they're detachable."

Kyle manages to unclip one. As it turns out, the pouch has a socket that connects to a nozzle on the suit.

"Let's see . . . The scrubber's portable vacuum backpack connects *here*—" Kyle points at a square hole at the back of a suit, and we peer in to see tubes that lead to each nozzle. "Okay . . . so the suit is designed to allow each pouch to fill up *one at a time*. But what if we use the suit in *reverse*?"

Kyle glances at a *REVERSE* button on the vacuum, then over at the brimstone chunk, and my eyes widen as I yelp, "*Whoa, whoa, whoa!* You want to turn a scrubber suit into an ash-spewing contraption?"

Her answer is a crooked smile.

Before I can respond, Kyle tells me to take off my scrubber suit and grab a fresh one. As I do so, she grabs a scalpel and then carefully cuts open the bag holding the brimstone.

The air suddenly reeks of cigarettes.

"Jas, take off all the pouches on both the new suits."

Jas? Is that what she used to call me?

Focus. I pour my attention into stripping away suit pouches, and when I'm finished, I've created a mound of twenty bags. That's when I notice Kyle using her scalpel to slice off tiny chunks of brimstone. We're running out of time, but she goes slowly. Careful not to create enough kinetic energy to, well, *blow up* the super carbon before we can use it.

Once she's cut twenty pieces, Kyle and I carefully place

one gray chunk in each pouch.

"Okay . . . that was the easy part," she whispers, before donning her new suit.

I do the same.

With a deep breath, we slowly clip our filled pouches onto the front and sides of our suits, then stick on our new helmets, followed by scrubber vacuum backpacks. Kyle and I take in a deep breath, waddle to the van's rear doors, and then exit with as little sharp movement as possible.

"Are we actually about to *invade* a VC building?" I whisper.

Kyle wavers but nods. "Sure. Why not? I mean, what've we really got to lose?"

We head to a nearby steel door that seems to lead into the building. I press a button next to it, but nothing happens. *Shit . . .* We need a key card.

Nearby, soldiers bustle around at another vehicle. One of them has a sharply pressed uniform studded with stripes and little badges. My heart skids when I realize it's Lieutenant Davey Shiner.

He'll notice us eventually. How could he not? In our scrubber suits, white against the gray-black walls, we look like fucking astronauts. I'm guessing this isn't the natural habitat of scrubbers.

Kyle gestures for me to face her. "We need to wait here for someone to trigger the door, so pretend we're talking. Try to act normal and not draw even more attention."

I want to say, *Okay*, but I'm too freaked about what

could happen if we're caught.

"Just . . . act natural," Kyle whispers.

"Act natural? And do what—*chitchat*?" I hiss.

That makes me think of the *one thing* I want to talk about: That memory from the pool. That suggestion that we were more than friends. I *know* we're thinking of the same thing.

Kyle moves closer and says, "Jasper, about the past . . . I promise I'll tell you everything later. Swear to God. But right now I need *you* to tell me something." She whispers even softer now: "I need you to tell me we're not gonna screw this up and end up dead or in a prison cell. Okay? Tell me we can do this."

I wish I could see her eyes through her visor.

"Can we do this?" I whisper. "Honestly? I dunno." My words falter, until I realize we're holding hands and making shapes that aren't shadows or mystery silhouettes from a photo. *We're* real. "Kyle . . . I'm not scared. Because even if this *is* the last thing we ever do, at least we're doing it together."

"Yeah?"

"Yeah. I *got* you." I keep holding her hands but sway from side to side. I tap my feet softly to the HVAC droning. "Ready to keep dancing in the chaos? And fighting?"

"Dancing and fighting? Like, capoeira?" she asks.

And when I laugh, she adds, "*Hell yeah*."

We let go of each other and try to look casual.

Shiner and his men head toward us, and I feel the weight of their stares.

"Apparently, there's a gene that determines the sort of earwax you produce," I tell Kyle, trying to make my voice sound unrecognizable and scratchy. "Did ya know there are *two* types of earwax? Dry and wet. How fascinating is that, Chen?"

Shiner flinches when he overhears my words, but he chooses to ignore us and unlock the door with his key card. He and his men enter, and we follow, casually, a few steps behind them.

Shiner and the soldiers enter an elevator hidden in a side wall, and I exhale in relief when the door closes and dings. Kyle whispers, "To use what we've made, grab your vacuum handle and press *REVERSE* on and off. That'll create a super-short burst of brimstone. Got it?"

"Got it," I whisper back.

We enter a foyer. Cold lights. High ceiling. Scientists in white lab coats. Steel doors along concrete side walls. Kyle walks to a wall-mounted plaque that has a building schematic, studies it, and then faces the center of the room. "On the count of three, shoot a pellet at the wall air vent to your left. I'll do the middle of the room. *One . . .*"

A distant receptionist gives us a pinched stare and says in a shrill voice. "*Eck-scuse me!* There are rules against scrubbers entering high-sec facilities!" People start to look our way.

"There are biohazard rules about—"

"We didn't ask for your rules!" Kyle yells as we whip out our vacuum handles.

We click our *REVERSE* buttons on and off and each blast out a chunk of brimstone. Mine lands on the left wall, roughly around the vent, and powderizes with a creepy *aahh*. Kyle's piece hits the ceiling. In an instant, everything becomes a gray murk, and all I can see are blurry silhouettes as soldiers and scientists stagger around, choking.

This ain't no capoeira. It's chaos.

Someone bumps into my arm, and I stumble backward, losing my bearings. "Ky . . . uh, *Chen!*" I call out.

"*Franklin!*" Kyle yells back. "This way!"

We Marco Polo our way to each other in a corner. Kyle grabs my hand just as Klaxons go off. "The ash has triggered the fire alarms!"

But instead of releasing water, metal spouts on the ceiling are gushing plumes of white gas. Were this a fire, the gas would've swiftly extinguished any flames, but here, now, all it does is churn the brimstone.

"*Damn*. Wasn't expecting that!" I shout. "Is this *safe* for people here?"

"I don't think it's enough to do serious damage to anyone," she replies. "But we don't exactly have time to check WebMD! We need to *move!*"

Kyle leads me to the left wall and feels around for a door. She tries the handle. Locked. But instead of freaking, she waits for a moment, and *click*, the fire safety system automatically unlocks all the doors.

We dart through the doorway, and the corridor beyond fills up with gray dust. I can barely see a dozen steps ahead of me, but I hold on to Kyle's hand as she leads the way.

I need to wipe my helmet panel every few seconds to clear my vision.

We get to a stairwell, and Kyle and I shoot pellets to clear the space ahead of us. Within moments, scientists and soldiers stagger out like animals smoked out from a hole. When we're reasonably sure everyone who's getting out has gotten out, we make our way down the stairs.

Sublevel 1 . . .

Sublevel 2 . . .

We get out at sublevel three and Kyle mutters, "This is it. The data archive level," before raising her vacuum spout. She's about to create a smokescreen.

But I hold her back. "No! We'll damage the computers!" I whisper, and she nods as we holster our vacuums. Only then do we gaze ahead at a corridor lined with identical steel doors.

Soldiers spot us and dart over, ready to tell us to halt. But Kyle doesn't hesitate as she shrieks out, "Ohmigod, ohmigod! Help! A demon chased us into the building! It's upstairs coughing up brimstone! Hurry!"

The guards race into the stairwell.

Once they're gone, we hurry down the corridor and find

a door marked *Science Research Archive.*

We head inside, and Kyle removes the black visor part of her helmet, revealing a clear screen behind it. I do the same, and we both slump to the ground with a huge, shared sigh. Her eyes are saucer-wide, but she pulls herself together to text Suckerpunch:

We're in.

16

UNIT 298

NOT BAD.

Those words flicker onto Kyle's phone screen before the Suckerpunch hacker reappears in his pixelated chat window. "Not bad at all," he echoes.

"What now?" I ask. No time to be clever. "We're in some sort of research archive."

"You're in a server room, to be precise," he says, and I look around at metal shelves with shoebox-sized gray boxes: computers without monitors.

"Look for a computer labeled UNIT 298. Once you find it, use a USB cable to connect the computer to Kyle's phone. That's how I'll access the unit."

"A USB cable? Shit, I don't have one!" says Kyle.

"On it," I tell them. "You find the computer; I'll get a cable."

I creep out into the corridor. My gaze catches sight of a door labeled *Kitchenette*, and I dart in. There's a microwave, a fridge, and over in a corner—*bingo!*—a phone connected to a charger via a cable.

When I return, Kyle is crouched in front of a computer labeled UNIT 298. I hand her the cable, she links her phone to the computer, and her phone screen flashes with the Suckerpunch logo. Footsteps sound in the distance.

"Hurry," I hiss.

"I'm inside UNIT 298," says the Suckerpunch guy. His pixelated face on Kyle's phone is replaced by a screen with a progress bar. "I'll need a few minutes to copy all the relevant info."

"Can we check the files while you copy them?" Kyle asks.

"Have a party," he replies distractedly.

The progress bar shrinks to a small strip as the phone screen scrolls through an alphabetical list of all the folders. Kyle navigates to *P*, where we see a folder labeled *Portal Closure*.

Inside the folder is one file: Portal_Closure_Experiments_Video_(45mins).mp4

Kyle hits *PLAY*, even though we have no time to watch the whole thing. She skips forward a few minutes, to a section where a bald scientist with round glasses stands in an empty room. He says, "Our Doomie subjects seem to have a strange relationship with the world beyond the portals—the *negative emotional plane*, as we refer to it—and these experiments aim to explore the connection between these unusual humans and the NEP."

"Doomies?" Kyle and I echo, swapping a gaze.

The scientist continues talking, and says, "When a Doomie claims to see the 'future,' I believe they are sensing the consciousness of the negative emotional plane . . . and what that consciousness is planning to do."

Kyle skips farther ahead.

Now the same scientist is standing in some abandoned office. There are soldiers in the background, but the camera-person follows the scientist as he heads closer to a portal—where a dozen Doomies in hospital gowns are standing just beyond a quarantine gate. They're shivering and doing their best to avoid looking at the hole.

"Easy, friends," the scientist tells them.

Kyle and I watch as he urges the Doomies to face the portal. "Remember what we discussed about your emotional clarity and sensitivity and depth—all the things that have caused you to be afflicted by Doomsday Delirium. Use that . . . *here*."

The Doomies close their eyes and sway as they seem to do something . . . with their minds? It's hard to tell.

Kyle skips ahead in the video. And that's when we see it.

The portal shivers, ripples, and then . . . spins inward.

Whoever's recording this staggers back and drops the camera. When the video reemerges, the quarantine zone is empty. No portal.

Kyle pauses the video.

"I've finished copying the files," says the Suckerpuncher.

Kyle doesn't seem to hear him as she turns to face me.

"This isn't just a high-security facility—it's also a *research* base," I seethe. "And that's why the asylum is located directly next door. So they can use Doomies for their experiments."

Kyle gives me a dazed look. "Jasper, we could close the mart portal if we had some Doomie backup." She says what I'm thinking: "We need to rescue as many as we can and get them to come with us."

"Can you help us?" I ask Suckerpunch.

After a pause he says, "A sky bridge connects the two buildings on level two. If you can cross over into the asylum, you could wreak some more havoc . . . and force the staff to release the Doomies from their cells."

"Good enough," says Kyle as she unplugs her phone and sticks it in her pocket. She puts her black visor piece back on, and so do I. "Okay! Let's give the folks over there a firsthand demo of the Dustbuster 4000!"

Kyle and I make it up to the second floor of the building only to find ourselves alone in a lab full of workstations and computers. Everyone seems to have been evacuated. Klaxons ring on.

"It's only a matter of time before VC backup arrives," Kyle mumbles as we linger.

I turn to face Kyle and write the word *Hey* in reverse on my dusty helmet screen.

She chuckles, less of a laugh and more of a shudder, but writes the same on hers.

"Ready?" I ask, to which she nods.

On the far end of the lab is a door slightly ajar. We go through it to enter a glass sky bridge that is ash-clouded on our side but clearer on the far end. We hurry across and peer through a glass door to see a medical waiting room. A couple of wheezing scientists with coats stained gray are being tended to by the asylum nurses.

We retreat a few steps until we're hidden again in the haze.

"How many rounds you got left?" she asks me.

"About six," I reply.

"Me too. When we get inside, flood the place with pellets. They'll be forced to evacuate everyone to the front lawn."

I'd ask her *Then what?* But we're clearly the poster children of making shit up as we go.

We barge into the asylum and fire away.

We didn't plan to attack Vanguard, but here we are, two Davids shooting stones at Goliath's crotch. And *man*, this somehow feels like we're evening a score. We holler as everything gets swallowed up in a soup of gray. Moments later we're all out of ammo.

"Okay, all the Doomies should be getting—"

Kyle doesn't get to finish that sentence. One moment she's standing in front of me, the next she's been pulled backward. A soldier has her by the backpack. She tries to fight him, but he flings her against a wall.

"No!" I yell out.

The soldier turns in my direction, and I see a familiar salt-and-pepper haircut.

It's fucking *Shiner.* He's wearing a gas mask and a pair of thick goggles.

"Show yourself!" he calls out to me.

I retreat into the shadows and look around for a weapon, but I can't see anything. *Think, think, think!* Then I realize that one of my suit pouches is still full.

Hell, yeah. I have one last pellet left.

I unclip this pouch, gently pour the brimstone onto my right hand, and carefully close my fingers around it before Shiner emerges from the fog.

"Take off your helmet. *Now,*" he commands, holding Kyle in a too-tight headlock.

When I waver, he squeezes Kyle tighter.

"Okay, okay! Chill!" I call out as I use my left hand to fiddle with my helmet. I make a show of it being jammed, and Shiner moves closer to me, ready to yank it off.

When he's directly in front of me, I throw a right hook at his face and punch him in the cheek before sliding my fist upward. I end up pushing away his goggles just as the brimstone in my grip powderizes in his face.

Shiner roars out. He lets go of Kyle and collapses.

"You okay?!" I ask Kyle as I help her up, but she doesn't answer. She just looks down at a writhing Shiner and kicks him hard in the side.

"Let's go!" she whispers.

Kyle guides me around a corner, then stops to take off her suit. I'm not sure what she has in mind, but I follow her lead. And as soon as my helmet is off, I feel like I'm breathing in—no, *drinking in*—an ashtray smoothie. I choke, then try breathing through my shirt collar as Kyle leads me into a stairwell full of Doomies.

We follow the crowd outside. Floodlights are on, but the afternoon sky might as well be night, and thanks to all the ash, Kyle and I are now as gray as everyone else. Her Kevlar vest is hidden under dust. Everyone looks . . . smudgy.

Kyle pulls out her phone and tells Suckerpunch, "We're out, along with the Doomies. What now?"

"Behind you is the eastern part of the fence," he says. "Sundown City reservoir is just a couple of yards beyond. If you can get to the reservoir, there are stormwater tunnels you can escape into."

"But how do we get through the fence?" I ask.

No answer. So Kyle says to me, "I'll work on the fence. You gather us some Doomies."

We split up, and I stumble around, looking for some Doomies who seem clearheaded enough. But all the Doomies are either catatonic or hallucinating.

"What have we done?" I whisper.

Only then do I see someone crouched to the side, hands to his head. I move closer and freeze. It's Pete Moretti. I kneel beside him as he tries distracting himself by reading the washing instructions tag on the hem of his medical gown: "'One hundred percent polyester . . . do not bleach . . . made in . . .'"

Carefully, I put a hand on his shoulder. "Pete. It's me . . . Jasper."

He looks up and blinks. "Jasper?"

"Come on. Follow me and I'll lead you out of this place."

Pete doesn't move.

"Buddy, we really need to go, like, *now*." I lean in closer and whisper, "We have a way to stop the *thing* you're always trying not to think about. But we need your help."

Pete still doesn't budge. "You can't stop *that*."

I blink. "Pete. We *can* do this. We can stop the end!"

Kyle's earlier theory returns to me.

"If we defeat *that stuff*, you won't have the nightmares and visions anymore! We'll be normal again. Free again to do whatever we want!"

No response.

"Pete. Help us stop a Black Friday disaster, and you'll live to see *Cyber Monday*. Just picture the discounted clothes you'll see on the VC auction app. There's no way Vanguard won't put *everything* on super sale!"

His eyes light up, and I get to my feet.

"Come on!"

He rises soon after. Only then do I tell him we need a dozen more Doomies. "The most clearheaded ones you know. Folks who can concentrate for long enough to get outta here."

"Okay!" he says with sudden pep.

"Okay." I smile back.

Pete stumbles off into the crowd. He gathers together ten young guys and girls, then comes back to my side. I tell them to follow me, and we head to the east side of the barbwire fence. Here, I find Kyle standing by a small gap on the fence's lower edge. She has carefully bent some spikes outward and is using her booted feet to kick the hole wider. Wordlessly,

Pete and I join her to help.

"Hey!" a soldier shouts out as he sees us.

He's too late. Kyle is already on the other side, holding up the wire edge for the rest of us. We scurry through to join her. The Doomies follow more quickly than I thought they could, and soon, we're running down a slope to reach a narrow ledge that runs along Sundown Reservoir.

Kyle chucks her heavy Kevlar vest and boots into the water, then leaps in. One by one we all follow. The Doomies seem unbothered, but the water is icy, and I can't feel the bottom. I flail about before I realize I *can* swim. Score one for me! Nice to have skills I didn't know I had. Kyle holds her phone above the surface, and we all hear the hacker dude tell us, "Swim to the other side, and climb onto the ledge there. Follow the path all the way to the reservoir opening. You'll see a gate in a wall."

Before long we've reached that barrier. It's secured by a combination lock, but the hacker guy gives us a four-digit code. Moments later, we've relocked the gate behind us, and we're running at top speed through a dark corridor, with only the light of Kyle's phone to guide us.

Suckerpunch leads us through a mazelike series of storm-water tunnels until we reach a wall-mounted ladder that leads up to a manhole cover.

Once more unto the breach, it seems. Once more.

17

ISO

We emerge in the middle of a suburban cul-de-sac surrounded by dead lawns and pale single-story houses. The rooftops and streetlights are covered in hanging strands that resemble silly string from a can—well, if silly string were as thick as pool noodles.

"Where are we?" I ask.

"Did we lose the VC?" Pete asks, looking over his shoulder.

Kyle holds out her phone, and the hacker says, "You're safe. This is the Suckerpunch HQ."

"This is an ISO," Kyle says as if it's obvious.

"A what?" Pete and I ask.

"An *isolated zone*. Some places that are too hard to restore—"

Kyle's phone dings. The hacker has sent a video clip of an enormous demonic aerosol can (with freaking *eyeballs*), and we watch it float above this neighborhood to spew out silly string everywhere. The video goes black when the person recording it gets crushed by a strand.

"*Insane*," Kyle says, shaking her head.

"When VC deems something irreparable, they just block it off with concrete walls to prevent people from getting close," says the hacker. At the same time, I hear his words mirrored in the distance, faintly. Is he nearby? "These houses still have running water, so you can use the showers to clean up. There's a lot of old canned food here too."

While he's talking, I wander off in the direction of his distant actual voice. What I find is a shadowed figure behind a yellow house, and this stranger startles, puts away his phone, and tries to climb over a fence.

"Wait!" I call out. "Hold on! I just want to talk."

He freezes but doesn't turn.

"Earlier you said 'long time no see.' Well, I have amnesia, so you should know I don't remember you—or much of anything, for that matter."

A long pause.

"I'm guessing we never met in person?"

His shoulders tense up before he slowly turns around.

"I'm Suckerpunch," he says as if that wasn't already obvious.

"Yeah, I get it, you're in Suckerpunch."

"No, dude, I *am* Suckerpunch. It's just me." He takes in a deep breath, moves closer, and I realize he's actually around my age. He's got short wavy hair, a coppery complexion, and huge bags below his eyes. He folds his arms and says, "So, now that we've helped each other out, I need you to leave as soon as possible."

"But," I object, "we're just getting started. The mission—"

"I'm not a Doomie. You don't need me."

He starts to wander off, so I say, "You can still be an honorary member of Team Doomie. We could really use your help—"

"Dude. I've got my own shit to worry about on Team *Me*."

He turns and slips away.

When I return to the cul-de-sac center, Doomies have already split into small groups to search the houses for food. Only Kyle remains, waiting for me on the dimly lit sidewalk. I wander over to her side, and for the first time in hours, we haven't got somewhere to run or something to do, and I find myself shivering until she bumps my shoulder with hers.

Wordlessly, Kyle leads me into a blue house that no one else has entered. There's no electricity, but over in a corner, a portable battery unit is hooked up to a lamp. In the weak light, we see a nearby Christmas tree surrounded by gift boxes in shiny wrapping. The family who lived here only unwrapped one present—a kid's toy truck—before Hell Portal Day unfolded.

I don't see claw marks or bloodstains, so I *think* we won't see any signs of casualties here.

Kyle and I head to a kitchen sink and use the running water to wash our arms, necks, and faces. We make mud in the sink. Moments later I find a phone charger and link my phone to a free socket on the battery unit.

As I turn to face Kyle, we *finally* have a moment to ourselves.

There's so much I want to say—

But the silence is punctuated by footfall from above. Fuck, we're not the only ones here. Kyle and I head cautiously upstairs, halting when we reach a room where someone's recently lit a candle on a table. We take in peach walls, shelves full of plush toys and figurines, and right ahead of us, there's Pete with his back to us.

He's swaying slightly, hands clutching his head, and my first thought is, *Is he on the verge of another Doomie vision? Was all this stress too much for him?*

"Pete?" I call out.

I move closer, then realize he's staring wide-eyed at some sweet fleece onesies that are strewn on a bed. Each one has a different color—red, blue, green. Pete turns to us and says, "Look! Aren't these freakin' amazing?" I notice some additional costume accessories: cowls with rodent ears; gloves and oversized feet made of beige fake fur.

I think these are costumes . . . for Alvin and the Chipmunks.

"Pete? That's someone else's stuff," I begin.

"It's not like they'll miss it," says Pete with a callousness that makes me flinch. He sees this and reddens. "Uh, that came out weird."

My hands clench as I take in wall photos of a teenage girl

with her parents. And I ask, "Pete. Did you lose anyone on Hell Portal Day?"

Pete lowers his head. "No."

"You're lucky, then," I mutter.

Curiously, *Pete* shoots me a stare as if to say, *No one here is lucky.*

Kyle places a hand on his shoulder. "Pete?"

When he doesn't answer, she whispers, "After Hell Portal Day, what happened to your family?"

Exhaling, Pete sits on the floor, picks at the carpet, and says, "Ever heard of the Preppers?"

We shake our heads as we kneel beside him.

"Well, the Preppers are folks who've been preparing for an apocalypse for, well, *decades.* I was raised in a prepper commune . . . and man, it was like being in a soul-sucking void. No one had nice things, or anywhere to call their own."

Kyle blinks. "Preppers? Wait! Are they those folks who only wear, like, potato sacks?"

Pete just turns to look at the elaborate onesies.

I blink. "Geez. What did they do in the wake of Hell Portal Day?"

"Well . . ." Pete rolls his shoulders. "All the Preppers retreated into a bunker, ready to live out their lives underground. But when I realized that the world *wasn't* actually over—just fucked up—I escaped and moved to Sundown City. And man, I *love it* out here." He relaxes his shoulders. "I know the world's a mess, but there's *freedom* in just living your life and dealing with whatever the fuck comes." He pats the onesies. "I like collecting new friends."

Pete's eyes glimmer as he brushes the fuzzy material, but Kyle says, "Pete. *Come on—*"

He gestures at the suits. "We should all put one on!"

Before I can argue, a grinning Pete puts a hand on our shoulders, and I find it hard to fight his mania. I turn to Kyle, expecting her to roll her eyes, but instead she says, "Fuck it. Dibs on the Simon one."

Her decisiveness makes me chuckle, but Kyle reddens and says, "*What?* Simon's the smart one." She hands me the Alvin suit and says, "Alvin's the rebel." She gives Pete the last one. "Theodore's the sensitive one."

Moments later, we've all donned costumes over our dusty clothes, and the only part of our bodies we can see are our faces. We laugh.

Seeing Kyle giggle—yeah, *giggle!*—makes me feel as though my now fleece-covered body could explode into tufts of fuzz. At least until I hear phone chimes coming from downstairs and realize my device must have gained enough power to turn itself on.

It keeps chiming over and over.

Kyle and I stumble downstairs, and I remove my furry chipmunk gloves in order to pick up my phone. I see tons of unanswered messages from Lara. Her latest one reads, **PICK UP! WHERE R U? YOU OK?!**

"Crap," I mutter to Kyle. "We forgot about Lara."

We peer back to check that Pete is still upstairs, then pick up the phone to video chat with Lara.

"Jasper! Kyle!" she yelps as her face appears. "Holy shit! I saw a Facebook post about an attack in the mart . . . I thought you were dead! Why the fuck are you dressed like chipmunks?"

We apologize to Lara, and start to recount what we experienced earlier. But before long she interrupts to say, "Whatever. Guys, there's something I need to tell you."

"What?" we ask.

"My connection to the abyss is weak, but the looming apocalypse has caused me to, like, *sense* the abyss again." Lara exhales shakily. "Earlier, I closed my eyes and saw the abyssals interacting with an army of demons. I saw the abyssals showing their monsters visions of Vanguard soldiers in action—"

Kyle shivers. "They want to train their demons to better combat the VC."

"To make them even more lethal so they can—"

Lara gets cut off when my phone goes flat again. I'm about to plug my phone back into the battery unit when Kyle says, "Look outside."

Peering out a window, I see portable outdoor lamps light up all around the cul-de-sac. There are dozens upon dozens of them, and they're each attached to a mini speaker that is now beeping.

"What's going on?" I ask Kyle.

"I don't know," she replies as we stagger out into the cul-de-sac.

Out of nowhere, Suckerpunch Dude appears in the open doorway of a yellow house on the far side. "Quick! Get your asses in here!"

"What's happening?" Kyle asks as we race over to the yellow house.

Suckerpunch says, "VC drones sometimes fly over. They use infrared to scan for heat signatures! The lamps are my early-warning system." He ushers us and the Doomies into a basement stairwell. "Come on! We have to go underground where it's shielded, or VC will detect life signs and swarm the zone."

I'm about to join the others in the basement but realize Pete is nowhere to be seen.

I race back to the blue house. I scamper up to that kid's bedroom, only to see him shifting additional onesies from a wardrobe and into a nearby suitcase. I yell at him to leave the stuff, but he keeps telling me, "One sec!"

I try to drag Pete toward the door, but he's surprisingly strong and holds his ground.

Kyle hurries to my side, stands between Pete and his suitcase, and shouts, "Pete! Come on! You don't need this stuff!"

"But—"

"You don't need pretend friends." Her voice softens. "You have *us* now."

I look to Pete. "Dude, come with *us*—the Unprepared. The—"

"The *This could go so badly, but let's do it anyway*—ers," Kyle adds.

"The Doomies!" I add.

Pete finally looks at us. Wavers. Nods. "*Right.*"

Shakily, he abandons his suitcase, and we all bound down into the cul-de-sac, where the beeping has evolved into a single keening note. And I'm guessing the drones are about to cross *directly* overhead.

"Crap!" Kyle hisses. "We won't make it to the basement!"

She's right. We're too far from the yellow house. But abruptly I see the Suckerpunch dude running up to us and we freeze. He unzips a backpack, yanks out a silver reflective blanket, and then tosses this fabric over him and us. "Stay low. Don't move!" he yells.

We huddle close.

None of us speak as we hear the drones fly onward into the distance.

A long minute later, the Suckerpunch guy throws off the cover, and we all stand to face one another, panting like we're about to keel over. That's when he extends a hand and says, "Uh, so yeah, I'm . . . Edwin."

"Hey, Edwin, nice to meet you," I reply, shaking his hand like we're about to become business partners. "So. Any chance you'll reconsider joining Team Doomie?"

He takes in our chipmunk outfits and mutters, "Ugh. Why do I feel like I'm gonna regret this?"

18

Kids of the Worst Places

After the chaos dies down, Kyle and I wander into the blue house's backyard, where we slump inside an empty inflatable pool that might as well be a raft adrift in shadows. Once again we've got a moment just to ourselves, but man, I have no idea how to focus all my questions about *us*. Yet *Kyle* is the one who finally breaks the tension.

"We should talk. . . . About the past, about you and me."

"Right," I whisper.

Kyle looks away, and all I can see is her silhouette in profile, until at last, she begins.

"Look, I've always been a loner. I love my family, but I've *always* preferred being on my own." She wraps her arms around herself. "When I was younger, it's like the whole world around me was a huge public swimming pool, full of splashing people, and all I wanted to do was sit on a far deck chair and read a damn book. I was always happy to hang back, not be a part of things.

"That's how I felt pretty much every day . . . until I met

you. It was freshman year. I was trying to find a seat in the cafeteria, and I saw you lingering in the exact opposite corner. Our eyes met . . . and I dunno, I just *knew*."

We've been drawn together so many times in the mart, by invisible strings. But *this* would've been the first tug.

"So we really had a past together?" I can barely breathe. "I have this photo in my room. I think it's us standing in front of a burning dumpster. . . ."

Her eyes light up. "Hah! That . . . Every Sunday we'd explore the *worst-ever places* in Sundown City—like, diners with one-star reviews, parks where people got mugged, a dumpster that was somehow always on *fire*."

"Why?"

"We were just being stupid," she tells me. "That . . . and also . . ."

"What?" I ask when she wavers.

"Well, ever since I was little, my folks would take me on road trips to see different colleges. I was, like, six and they already wanted to inspire me to get into the 'best places ever.' But I never wanted to live the American dream. Not like they did. They wanted me to dive into that metaphorical public pool, but man, all I wanted was to stare at the *ocean*." She looks to me. "We *both* wanted *something else*."

"I didn't want to go to college?"

"Nope. It was like everyone was telling us, 'Work hard! Go to a great college or your lives will be shit!' So . . . we ended up seeking out 'worst places ever' in order to see up close what that shit was like. Sort of our way to tell everyone to back the fuck off and let us make our own choices. But then, well, everything changed after . . ."

Hell Portal Day.

Kyle places a hand on my shoulder. "I'm so sorry about what happened to your parents." I don't know what to say, but I place my hand over hers. There's a heavy pause before she continues, "After they died, you withdrew from everything. And it all got worse after the subway attack."

"I got attacked on the subway?"

Kyle pulls her hand away and swallows hard.

"A year ago, we were on a subway platform when a demon broke through a portal zone. The fucker was a beachball with eyes all over it. It chased people in the station and smashed into them to just—" She makes an explosion gesture with her hands. "We were stuck in a corner, and we *would've* died. . . . Like, it was coming *right* for us. But this beefy Vanguard soldier used a razor sword to slice it in half."

My heartbeat is pounding in my ears.

"After that, I started thinking about enlisting in Vanguard, while you . . ." Kyle looks away into the shadows. "You got really fucked-up and angry. You couldn't accept how everyone was so willing to follow VC and carry on in the chaos. It wasn't long before you started looking for people who felt the same way as you."

"Which led me to find Suckerpunch?"

Kyle nods. "Yeah. Before long, you were tumbling down their conspiracy-theory rabbit hole." She leans forward to rest her elbows on her knees, head lowered. "We began drifting apart, and when I actually *did* enlist in Vanguard, we got into a terrible fight."

Kyle looks away, breathes slowly like she's trying her best to hold her composure. "I said things that I didn't mean. Made it seem like I wished we'd never met."

Before I can process that, she says, "We broke up shortly after. But then, a few weeks later, I was randomly assigned to the mart, and I didn't know about your amnesia. So when you said, *Hi. I don't think we've met*—"

"You thought I was fulfilling your wish?"

She nods. "I couldn't handle it. It seemed so mean."

Kyle finally looks at me, and I almost think she's bracing for the blow-up pool to disappear, along with the ground. I reach out to wrap my arms around her. "I'm sorry," I tell her. "I didn't know."

"I'm sorry too," says Kyle, looking into the dark. "I should've told you about *us* the moment I learned about your amnesia. But . . . I guess I felt that we were just doomed to fall apart." She swallows a lump before quickly adding, "You know, because of Hell Portal Day and the chaos, blood, and everyday nightmare of our world. But now, I think maybe I was afraid to let myself hope for anything."

"I know what *that* feels like," I tell her.

I squeeze her tightly. My head zings, and I realize I'm

trying to remember something from my past. Anything about Kyle and me.

The zinging turns to blackness.

"*Jasper!*" I hear Kyle yelp, but she sounds a million miles from me.

When I come to, I've rolled out of the inflatable pool and onto the ground. Kyle is kneeling beside me, helping me up, as I explain in a daze that "this happens every damn time I try to remember my past."

Her eyes go wide. "Well, maybe it'd be best if you don't focus on the past right now. We've got a shit ton to do—if we want to, you know, save the world and all."

Before I can respond, the streetlights around us flicker on with a soft hum, seemingly on some city-grid timer. We get up as the neighborhood fills with a grayish light. But seconds later, the giant silly strings drink up this streetlight and convert it into florescent colors. Shimmering hues that turn the rundown houses and dried lawns into an alien landscape.

"This *has* to be another awesome worst place ever, right?" I whisper.

Kyle reaches for my hand, and I think of what she said about us wanting to find our own way in a world that wasn't ours. It dawns on me now that our paths have led us right here, right back to each other.

Her hair is stardust. "What're you thinking?" she asks quietly.

"I just . . ."

I lean closer to try to kiss her. But . . . my lips land between her nose and upper lip. I laugh softly, then realize I'm blowing a warm breath in her face.

Kyle chuckles too as she pulls away. I can see alien colors reflected in her eyes, like sparklers. Our lips finally connect. Her lips, hands, hair—every bit of her might as well be made of light. My head and shoulders tingle and burn.

Only then do I know what this feeling is.

We were more than a couple. We were in love.

Holding on to her, two words echo in my mind.

Still are.

In my dreams, I'm standing alone in the mart, the halogen flickering, the PA buzzing with static. *Where is everyone?* I walk through the nearest aisle and nearly slip on a wet floor. What I suddenly realize isn't water . . . but blood.

Shit! Shit! Shit!

Footsteps echo behind me, and I turn to see four humans stalking toward me, their bodies obscured by the dimness. Before I can retreat, they're only a few steps away, and one thought echoes: *Horsemen.*

They lunge, and one gets close enough to place a hand on my shoulder. The skin-to-skin contact causes an energy pulse to flood into my body, and it *burns.* I scream and tumble to the ground, and just as my head melts from the inside, one thought roars through my mind:

Powers! They'll have superpowers.

19

Thanksgiving

The next morning, Edwin wakes us all and leads us down into the yellow house's basement. The ceiling is lined with aluminum foil to block infrared drone scans, and it gives the place a snazzy, nutjob disco vibe. The walls are festooned with LCD screens, each scrolling with computer code, and the worktables are littered with half-finished projects.

Edwin gestures at cereal boxes on a table. "It ain't much, but if you're hungry . . . ," he says, before he gets lost in an electrical project on a workbench.

Kyle stuffs a handful of Frosted Flakes into her mouth as she takes in the room.

"You okay?" I whisper.

"Last night, I had this dream. I saw . . . I saw a . . ." She falls silent, and somehow I think she saw the same dream as me. But I'm not ready to dwell on that just yet.

Pete comes over to say hello. Unlike Kyle and me, he's *still* wearing his Chipmunk onesie (albeit without the furry gloves). He proceeds to introduce us to the asylum Doomies. The chattiest one is Becky, a girl with a blond buzz cut, who behaves as though we're all just strangers sharing a holiday Airbnb.

Becky says to Edwin, "So! This is where you do your, uh, Suckerpunching?"

Edwin doesn't look up as he tinkers with the electronics inside some kid's plastic toy. He says, "Suckerpunching? You mean, cable hacks that I cast out through a series of untraceable proxies to over a hundred different screens across the city at a single go? Yeah, this is where I do my 'suckerpunching,' I guess."

Edwin finishes tweaking the toy. It's a six-inch-tall plastic figurine of a standing Alvin Chipmunk. He closes up a panel at the back.

Pete says, "Gah! That's super cute!"

"Say hello to the Hell Sniffer 8000," Edwin says with a shrug.

"The what?" says Kyle.

Edwin holds the figurine horizontally, and there's a light bulb embedded in the top of Alvin's head. It's a flashlight. He switches it on, but no glow appears. At least, not until Edwin aims the bulb at a nearby jar that contains a *demon talon*. Only then does it light up.

"The Hell Sniffer contains experimental VC tech that I stole. Its sensors can detect energy from the *other side*." Edwin waves the Hell Sniffer around, revealing that the Chipmunk has a tiny, focused range. "Yeah. It's kinda useless unless you're, like, three feet away from a demon, and facing it front on."

Edwin turns it off. I try to step closer for a better look, but something crunches under my feet. I look down to see empty pill bottles with the label Modafinil. Each is prescribed to a different person.

"What the heck is this?" I mumble.

Kyle crouches beside me and says, "Modafinil's meant to fight narcolepsy. But VC forces guards to take these when they're doing superlong shifts." She shakes her head at the sight of several dozen bottles. "However . . . there's a limit to how much a person can take."

"I use it to stay awake," Edwin mutters. "I need to watch everything VC is doing."

One of the bottles is large enough to have side effects printed on the label—*irritability . . . anxiety . . . depression . . . paranoia.*

"Gimme that," Edwin says, swiping the bottle out of my hand. "While you were lying around, I watched *all* the video material that we stole and indexed the sections."

Edwin places his laptop on the table. Kyle, Pete, and all his friends start crowding around the screen, just as someone calls my phone.

I pull it out to see a video call request from Lara.

Lara should see what secrets we've uncovered, in case she has insights, so I press *ACCEPT.* Her face pops up on my phone. "Hey, Jasper!"

Her voice draws the attention of the others, and I'm reminded that they don't know about her. *Crap.* "Uh, I need to introduce you all to someone, but I want you to stay calm and not freak when you meet her. She's . . . not quite human."

"Not quite human?" repeats Becky.

"Well, she's . . . a demon," I reply.

Pete and his friends flinch as I try to explain. "She's on our side, helping us learn about the forces beyond the portals, and she's . . ." I decide to change tack. "Her name is Lara. She loves pizza, *Friends* reruns, and wants to live her life—just like you and me."

"Can we . . . see her?" Pete asks.

Here goes nothing . . .

I show them my phone. Lara tips her head to the side, waves cutely, and the people around me relax a little as she turns on her usual charm.

"How you folks doing? I'm Lara. Uh . . . Happy Thanksgiving, everyone!"

Thanksgiving? Right, of course.

The day before Black Friday.

The Doomies take a few moments to say hello to Lara before I point my phone back at Edwin's laptop. "Lara, there's some stuff here you should see too," I tell her, before nodding at Edwin to hit *PLAY*.

"You sure she's cool?" Edwin asks, and I nod and tell him, "Yeah. I'm sure."

The first section of video shows an unconscious Doomie girl strapped to a gurney next to a portal. The bald scientist shakes her to wake her up. She looks around, sees the portal and soldiers, and gets super agitated. As she trembles, so too does the portal. Seconds later, the portal spews a six-feet-tall spider made of camo material, which takes three guards to slay.

The next few minutes of video show a supercut of similar

experiments. Doomies in distress seem to trigger portal chaos. All the while, the scientist guy narrates: "We've known for some time that portal creatures are influenced by human fears and nightmares. But the frequency and timing of invasions has been almost impossible to predict. However . . . when 'Doomies' stand close to a portal, they sometimes have the ability to interact with the world on the other side—and the most emotional, most turbulent Doomies can trigger *immediate* creature events."

Edwin pauses the video and says, "*There.* Proof that Doomies can cause heightened portal chaos."

My thoughts go to the aftermath of the eye-monster attack: Kyle's extreme emotion when she saw me injured. Was *that* what caused the portal to suck us in?

Kyle glances at me, pales.

"I heard rumors in the asylum that the doctors once used Doomies for experiments," Becky breathes. Her chipperness has melted, and her arms are wrapping around herself like she wants a straitjacket that's no longer there.

Edwin plays another section.

Four blindfolded Doomies are standing next to a portal lodged in the wishing well of an abandoned mall. They don't seem to know where they are. The portal quivers slightly, but then the scientist starts playing some old-time pop song and just like that, the Doomies relax. And slowly the portal stops trembling.

The video cuts to a clip of the scientist addressing the

camera: "As you can see, positive stimuli *can* also have an effect on the Doomies' power. Behold, these extraordinary results—" The video cuts to a close-up photo of the wishing-well portal, with the label *BEFORE*.

The next photo is labeled *AFTER*, and it shows the same portal from the same angle, but this time, the opening is a little smaller—not by a lot, but the change is distinct.

Pete and his friends look at each other with wide eyes, before Edwin skips to—

A video set in an empty underground parking lot, where a dozen Doomies are standing in a circle around a portal. They stare right into the hole. It trembles as if echoing their fear. But the scientist gets them to hold hands, and says, "*Remember* . . . Focus your positive emotions at the portal." He pauses to eye them all. "If you need something to feel positive about—remember our deal."

"Deal?" I echo.

Edwin mutters, "The scientist promised to release them if they succeeded in this experiment."

We watch as the portal starts swirling, first slowly, then faster and faster, a liquid shadow going down an invisible sink, until there's . . . *nothing*.

The Doomies around me are cheering and hooting, and somehow our bodies almost seem to *radiate* a warm energy that cocoons around us. But I turn to see Kyle's gaze fixed completely on the screen.

The video abruptly skips ahead. To a piece where the

cameraperson seems to be shooting in secret from behind a concrete pillar. I can just see the lead scientist talking to Lieutenant Shiner.

The latter says, "This is not up for discussion. For the security of Vanguard, you will cease your experiments *immediately*. All material is to stay classified."

The video file comes to an end, and Edwin says, "Surprise, surprise. VC doesn't want anyone to know that the world might actually be *fixable*!"

"What happened to those Doomies?" Kyle asks. "Did they get freed in the end?"

Edwin wavers. "Um. Well . . ."

Silence fills the room. The warm energy evaporates into nothing.

I step away from the laptop to look at my fellow Doomies. "Guys, we can shut the mart portal *before* Black Friday. We can forever lock out the abyssals from coming into our world. We can do this!"

I look at Kyle, who tries matching my smile. "Right," she agrees, nodding. "But we'll need to practice before we go to the mart. We're only going to get one shot at this, so we better be ready." She turns to Edwin. "Can you help us?"

"What do you need?" he asks.

"A training zone."

Edwin leads us to the manhole we emerged from, then uses a crowbar to lift the cover, and says, "There's an outdoor portal that you could try to affect."

"Is anything alfresco really a good idea?" I ask.

"Better than indoors," he replies, as if it's blindingly obvious, before climbing down into the stormwater tunnel below.

Kyle and I swap a shrug before following the other Doomies down. Edwin leads the way, confidently following turns that I can't imagine anyone being able to remember by heart. Grates and drains let in slivers of light from above, but there are long stretches where the stormwater tunnels might as well be the city's hollow bones. The sounds of cars above are a distant, arrhythmic heartbeat.

Eventually, Edwin needs a break to catch his breath. Some of us take the time to chat softly. Becky wants to speak to Lara, who is still on video chat. She has questions about hell—and Lara enlightens Becky, Pete, and the others about the abyss and the abyssals.

And I'll give them this: they seem comforted finally knowing the truth.

Edwin is about to signal us onward when his phone chimes.

"Problem?" Kyle asks.

"An alert. I've got a program that scans VC comm bands for interesting chatter." Edwin pulls out his phone and clicks a button to show us a screen that reads, DECRYPTING...

A few seconds later, we see a fragment of a video transmission from a grizzly-looking Vanguard officer. He's standing in a morgue beside a huge mound of body bags. "Sir, I don't think we can keep covering up the huge spike in attacks. These last few hours have been insane—"

The video ends.

No one makes a sound, until Lara breaks the silence: "The abyssals are sending out more demons than ever. They're getting bodies lined up for them to inhabit."

Before we can let *that* sink in, Edwin says, "We better keep going."

A short while later, the tunnel ceiling is so low that we need to crawl. I look back to see Pete struggling to keep up as he tries not to get his onesie grubby. Only now do I notice something sticking out of a pocket in his side—the Chipmunk head of the Hell Sniffer 8000.

Pete follows my gaze and reddens. "Well, it's the *perfect* accessory to finish this look," he whispers.

I chuckle softly but whisper, "*Pete.* Give it to me. I'll go return it."

Pete wavers for a long moment but eventually hands it over. "I was just borrowing it."

I put the Hell Sniffer into my pocket, then crawl after the others, just in time to find that everyone has stopped near a drain panel cut into the edge of a sidewalk. We stare out it like it's a periscope to see the opposite sidewalk, where a portal quarantine is located within an alleyway. One guard is stationed in the quarantine zone, while another stands outside.

"This is it," says Edwin. "A portal just a couple of yards away. Is this close enough?"

"Might be," I reply. And I'm about to ask the group for suggestions on how to project our "powers," until I realize they're all looking to *me*. "Uh, okay. I guess we should—"

Should what?

"Aim positive emotions at the portal."

"Positive emotions?" Pete echoes.

I think of the videoed Doomies who closed a portal and how they were inspired by the promise of freedom. "Picture the future you'd like to see. Imagine all the awesome things you'd like to experience after we stop the apocalypse. And, I dunno, just cast that energy toward the portal."

"Maybe close your eyes to concentrate?" Edwin suggests.

My fellow Doomies close their eyes. I do the same, and I imagine a future where Kyle and I are sitting inside a VW van, me behind the wheel, Kyle next to me with her window rolled down, her hair blowing about as we soar down an open road, headed for nothing but the gold horizon. I picture Kyle laughing and smiling at something I've said.

Joy rises inside me.

This might be the most glorious thing I've thought of in a long time. But it's weird. It's like I'm watching a film instead of imagining my life, so I try to visualize myself in a first-person POV behind the wheel. And just like that, the whole scene disintegrates.

I . . . don't get it.

"It's not working," says Becky. I open my eyes to see her staring out through the drain grate.

Pete shakes his head. "Maybe it's too hard to really find good thoughts."

I keep trying to picture myself *in* that van, on that road trip, but something inside me keeps blocking me. And I think I know why. "It's terrifying . . . ," I whisper, maybe to us all. "Terrifying to dare dream that things might work out, when we all know how fucked-up things are in this world. Like, who the hell are *we* to expect anything to change, or get better? It's all too much."

No one says a word, but I *know* they understand me.

Lara calls out to us, "I have an idea."

I'd forgotten she was still on video chat. She says, "Guys, I've seen enough *Friends* episodes to know what Thanksgiving is about." When we don't say a word, she adds, "Come on, everyone! If the future seems overwhelming, then focus on the *present*. Think of what you're grateful for . . . and use *that* joy!"

I'm not sure how that'll be powerful enough, but I whisper, "What am I thankful for?"

I reach out for Kyle's hand, and she squeezes my palm tightly as she gazes back.

"I'm thankful for *us*."

I use my free hand to hold Pete's, and all of us Doomies link hands as we echo our gratitude for one another.

A shudder passes through the group. My fellow Doomies

seem to fall into a trance, their eyes staring into space, as though their minds have gone somewhere else. Somewhere I've yet to follow. I'm about to try joining their trance until I hear a humming in the distance and peer through the drain grate. Over in the quarantine zone, the portal is shivering and buckling. . . .

And then—*poof*—it dissolves into nothing.

Edwin gasps loudly, breaking the spell that had fallen over everyone. The portal guards are startled. "What the fuck just happened!" one of them yells.

Edwin pulls us away from the drain grate and leads us to a wider tunnel a dozen yards away, where we can stand upright. "We did it!" Kyle and Becky both yelp.

They did. I wasn't as powerful as the others.

But before I can dwell on that, Lara cheers through my phone. "You guys did it!"

"It was your suggestion, Lara."

"Gratitude is an awesome shortcut to joy," says Lara. "I heard it in a TED Talk."

Before I know it, we're all huddled together, even Edwin, and Kyle says, "We're as ready as we're going to be! Let's go to the mart and shut the aisle nine portal *today*."

Edwin nods. "Okay, this way—"

As he tries to get his bearings, a dark shape flickers to my right. The shape stretches toward us, and I realize it's actually a person's shadow.

Lieutenant Shiner bursts into the light and grabs the

nearest Doomie. She shrieks, but he Tasers her to the ground. Five other soldiers materialize behind him. Doomies scatter but don't get far as flashes of electricity shred the dimness.

Kyle, Edwin, and I race in the opposite direction.

No, no, no! I mouth.

"Follow me!" Edwin hisses, retreating into the shadows.

The soldiers seem to think they've got all the Doomies, and we peer carefully around a corner to watch in horror as the VC forcibly drags the Doomies away. I hear Pete crying out into the dark. Over in a corner, a hulking soldier wavers near a cowering Becky and says to her, "Hey . . . *Get up.*"

When Becky refuses to rise from a fetal position, Shiner jabs the soldier sharply on the shoulder and barks an order at him to get her moving. The soldier *kicks* Becky and hauls her to her feet by the collar of her shirt.

Kyle pulls me back before anyone can see me. But in doing so, the Hell Sniffer 8000 falls out of my pocket and thuds onto the ground. I quickly grab it back, but the soldiers must have heard the clatter. Their voices hush.

Footsteps head our way.

"They're coming!" Kyle whispers.

We race ahead, and the passage forks into two shadowy tunnels. We go left, only to run into a bricked-up dead end. Just then, Shiner's voice echoes from the wider passage: "Attention! It's time to go back into your fucking cages, kids." In the dim light, I can see Shiner approaching—his right eye bloodshot, his left covered in an eye patch. He'll be at the fork in moments. "I've spent all day searching for you. You *do not* want to waste another moment of my time."

"What do we do?!" I whisper to Kyle.

She doesn't say a word.

Shiner's shadow creeps along the wall beyond our tunnel, but Edwin just whispers, "When I create a distraction, run straight ahead and then take a left."

"Edwin—"

"You're our only chance!" Edwin whispers as he unzips his bag to pull out a flare gun. He races out into the wider passage and fires the flare. The space floods with smoke and light.

The smoke instantly stings my eyes. My vision becomes a sea of red. Kyle senses this, grabs my hand, and guides me through the tunnel beyond. I can barely breathe, but I can hear the sound of footfalls getting closer.

"Down!" Kyle hisses.

We crouch. The corridor here has a huge pipe that runs along the lower part of a wall, and under this pipe, Kyle says, is a gap. Wordlessly, we both slip underneath the pipe, our bodies parallel with the wall, her boots touching my shoulders.

I can feel Kyle shaking as the soldiers charge through the corridor, flashlight beams searching the terrain. But there's enough smoke in here to shield us, keep us safe.

The footsteps recede into the distance.

We stay motionless until we finally get back our courage.

I rise to my knees, but *I* can't stop shaking. "The others. We've got to free them!" I tell Kyle, who's motionless.

She shakes her head. "We . . . can't save them."

"But we got them into this—"

"*Jas*, we have to get somewhere safe before Shiner and those soldiers double back." She grabs my hand, and I realize she's trembling just as hard as me. But in her eyes, I see a steadiness as she says, "We have to get outta here. Or there'll be *no one* left to stop the horsemen."

Finally it sinks in. It's all on us now.

Somehow, we manage to get far from any sign of Shiner and his men, but we end up stuck in a concrete labyrinth where the tunnels are barely four feet high, lit only by a weak glow from the narrow drain slats overhead. Time gets smudgy. But just as I start to worry we're going in circles, we come across a manhole and are able to emerge in a run-down part of Sundown City. It's a place with tents everywhere, mounds of garbage moldering, and not a single VC patroller in sight. It's a forgotten slum where no one takes notice of two dirty, sweaty kids.

"Where are we?" Kyle breathes.

My gaze takes in a black sky. "Oh God. It's . . . night already," I whisper. "We're running out of time. . . ."

At midnight, Black Friday begins.

"We need a place to crash, so we can figure out what to do." Kyle points out a distant metal structure. "That's the

Sundown City bridge. Your apartment should be near there."

I pull out my phone and GPS a course back to my place.

It's quiet on the way. No VC. Even though Shiner and his men didn't get a clear look at our faces, we keep our heads low as we enter a better district full of CCTV cameras. We walk as fast as we can, until eventually, we get to my apartment building and scamper up the back stairwell.

Once we're in my place, we crumple down against the front door. Lara rushes over and climbs onto my lap. "Jasper! What happened? The video cut out all of a sudden!"

"The other Doomies. They're . . . gone."

Her eyes widen. "All of them?"

I nod.

"But . . . How will we . . ." Lara falls silent before she can finish her question. She presses her body against my chest, and I wrap one arm around her, the other around Kyle. None of us speak as we stare at a wall clock behind my parents' TV: 9:45 p.m.

Two hours left.

Kyle pulls free and kneels in front of us and says, "We can't give up."

"Dude, we're cooked," I reply. "It takes a dozen Doomies to close a portal. We don't have the manpower anymore."

"So then we *don't* close it," she says, a wild look in her eye.

"What?"

"We search the mart for the horsemen." Kyle turns to Lara and says, "I know you said the horsemen will have blended in among humans. But is there *any* way to identify them if they're close enough?"

Lara shakes her head. "I can't track their energy."

My shoulders straighten as I reach into my pocket for the Alvin Chipmunk flashlight. "We do have Edwin's Hell Sniffer—"

I turn it on, aim it at Lara, and the bulb atop Alvin's head glows.

Her tail flicks as her eyes gleam. "That thingamabob can detect energy from the abyss? Damn!"

I pull back the Chipmunk and cause it to darken. "The range is way narrow."

"But it's our only hope," says Kyle. "We'll look for suspicious humans that might actually be horsemen, then use the Hell Sniffer for instant confirmation."

"Okay. But after we find them? What then?" I ask.

Kyle doesn't waver. "I don't think we have any other choice: we kill them."

The three of us cram down some leftover pizza as we mull what we have to do. "What do you know about abyssal powers?" I ask Lara.

"Abyssal powers? I fuckin' hate their powers," says Lara with a shudder. "Back in the abyss, the abyssals are always inflicting their powers on demons. Like, I've seen them turn demons into puppets. Seen them cause demons to literally turn *inside out*." She's trembling. "Life in the abyss was . . ."

When Lara goes silent, I gently rub the back of her neck. "You're here now, Lara. You're safe."

Lara gives me a look that says, *Yeah, but for how long?*

I quickly ask, "So. What powers will the *horsemen* have?"

The cat shrugs. "There's no way to know. But the horsemen will each have a power related to whatever emotion they embody."

Kyle scoots closer and finally tells us about her dream from last night. "I basically saw a horseman drive people insane just by touching them."

"Wow, yeah. I forgot to mention: they need to physically *touch* you to exert their power," says Lara. "So try not to get too close to them."

I think of how we'll surely get smooshed by huge Black Friday crowds.

Kyle must be thinking the same thing, because she says, "We'll just have to plan for the worst, hope for the best."

Soon after, Lara climbs up into my backpack, and the three of us head out. As we wander our way onto the street, Lara whispers, "Time?"

"Ten forty-five," I reply.

One hour and fifteen minutes left . . . until we save the world or watch it fall to pieces.

Black Friday

Lara, Kyle, and I make our way carefully through downtown, where despite VC's prohibition on sleeping in the streets, the sidewalks are filled with sleeping bags and tents. People are desperate to be first in line to grab the best deals.

Several VC soldiers head over, and I worry we're about to be plucked until I see a soldier help an old lady to open a folding chair. He tells her, "Have a nice Black Friday, ma'am." Kyle's phone chimes, and she shows me a text message from Vanguard: **ATTN SOLDIERS. Remember to SMILE today and be as helpful as possible. -VC MGMT.**

Soldiers are marching single file down the sidewalks, and it hits me that today is Vanguard's time to justify all their bullshit. They couldn't heal the world, but they've helped people stay drugged out on mindless distractions.

"Let's keep going before VC cannons start shooting Walmart coupons," I mutter.

It's 11:10 p.m. when we get to the mart. There's a line of people outside the front doors. "Could one of these folks be a horseman?" I ask Lara, who's in my backpack.

214

"Unlikely," she replies. "Look at how anxious they are. These people came to shop."

"Right," I mutter. "So we should be on the lookout for anyone who isn't shopping or behaving like a shopper." Good news, since I'm familiar with almost every animal found in the safari known as Retail.

We head to the rear staff entrance and use it to enter the back room. Kyle goes to the VC inventory room to get a new uniform and a flamethrower, while I head to a quiet corner with discarded boxes. I find an empty eight-inch square box, use my fingers to poke a small hole in the front, then slip the Chipmunk flashlight inside. I line up the bulb with the hole.

After that, I take off my backpack and pull out Lara.

"What's the box for?" Lara whispers.

"Discreet portable scanner," I reply, holding the small box under my left arm and Lara in my right. "Now, time to get *you* set up. Before someone sees us."

I hurry to the aisles and carefully toss Lara up onto the top of the toy aisle, where she can hide amid a display of plush animals. I'm alone here, so I call up to her, "Can you see the whole store?"

"Sort of," she replies.

Good enough. Kyle and I will check in with her every few minutes, and I'm guessing there'll be so much chaos that no one's going to notice us talking to a plushie.

When I return to the back room, Kyle beckons me away from the nearby staff and over to the moldy storeroom from the other day.

Once we're inside, door closed, Kyle looks at the box and says, "Good thinking." She pulls out a VC walkie-talkie—a small three-inch unit, just like the one clipped to her vest shoulder pad. She pins this on the inside of my work vest and says, "This comm is linked to mine. Press the top button to talk, the bottom to receive. It'll beep when one of us comms the other."

Kyle puts a gun in my free hand.

I flinch. "Seriously? I've never—"

"Don't worry. It's easy." Kyle shows me how to turn off the gun's safety mechanism, then how to hold it, and says, "Remember, don't yank on the trigger. Squeeze it."

I nod and shove the gun into my pants pocket. The weight of it is hard to ignore.

After a long pause, Kyle says, "Anything you wanna say before shit gets crazy?"

I once saw a VC soldier make the sign of the cross before entering this place. I'm not religious, but right now I wish I had a prayer to say. But instead, what pops into my head is what Gutierrez told me a VC recruiter said at our graduation:

"'What more can school teach you? You know as much about survival in a broken world as any adult. You know shit all.'"

"You remembered that?" Kyle asks.

Instead of explaining, I tell her, "I get it now. We don't need anyone to teach us a damn thing. We're learning about the world in the only way that matters—by being *in it*. That's why we *do know* shit. About survival. About laughing through all the crap. About *living*." I step closer. "We fucking got this."

Kyle leans forward to kiss me.

When we pull away, she says, "Let's do this."

We head into the back room again, just in time to see clerks gathering in the loading zone. Kyle gets called away to join a nearby group of guards; Gully catches sight of me and waves me over. He gestures for us to squish in closer and says, "Okay! Listen up, turds! Black Friday's about to begin, and I expect you all to be on your best fucking behavior. And FYI, I've locked up the back exit . . . so don't even *think* about sneaking off early."

It's 11:58 p.m. The mart doors are locked.

Hundreds of shoppers are massed outside the store, cheeks pressed to the glass, and I'm reminded that some of the worst demons don't have fangs or claws, but loyalty cards.

Gully calls out, "Activate the sliding doors and roll out the red carpet! It's go time!"

With the flick of a switch, the store opens and an ocean of humanity spills through the entrance.

"Here we go," I tell Kyle via our comm.

Shoppers crush past, clutching gaming consoles as though the boxes were life preservers. People carry flat-screen TVs above their heads with a strength I'm sure they didn't know they had until they saw the sale price.

I climb up a wheelable ladder to get a better view of the action. I spy butt cracks galore as people bend down to grab stuff off shelves. The metal trough of DVDs—which I thought was bolted to the ground—is moving amid the crowd like a barge.

A dozen feet away, two girls film two grandpas fighting over a jumbo crate of Tang. (Who even *wants* that much Tang?) A giant of a woman grabs on to my wheeled ladder and begins pushing it toward the checkouts. "Ma'am! This isn't for sale!"

The woman looks up, sees me, thinks for a second longer than I'd expect, then says, "I don't want that" and wanders off.

Kyle has taken position on top of a crate near aisle four. "Jasper! Focus."

Right. I try to look for folks who are not shopping, not jostling, not screaming, not cheering. Eventually, I realize I'm too conspicuous on the ladder, so I reach into my box and turn on the flashlight, then head down into the fray.

"You never know, Jasper," I mumble as I hold the device in front of me and let it scan the three feet space ahead. I might get lucky and pick up a signal. With that, I step farther into the crowd. And . . .

Big mistake. Shoppers rush at me with ridiculous questions. "Does that forty percent discount on pet food apply to people food?" "Where is aisle seven?" (*Uh, between aisles six and eight.*) "Do I have enough VC credits to afford this new stereo?" I try my best to answer while I push through the crowd, trying to find anyone who might be giving off Horseman of the Apocalypse vibes.

The crowd is starting to seem like a *Where's Waldo?* book but instead of Waldo, I'm looking, you know, for heralds of doom. "Anything, Lara?" I call up to the cat once I'm in the toy aisle.

"Nup!" she replies, shouting to be heard over the din. "Nothing so far."

In the security mirror, I catch a glimpse of the clothing section, where some people are trying on clothes right there on the spot. They're literally getting naked in public to see if a ten-dollar pair of jeans fits.

"Kyle, I don't see anyone who's not shopping," I whisper into my comm.

Kyle slips away from her area of duty to tell me in person, "It already feels like the end of the world out here."

This place would definitely top our list of best worst places.

Standing by the back room entrance, Gully peers around the store, clapping. I remember the Black Friday Bonus Bonanza challenge that he's hell-bent on winning.

"Stay focused. Things could turn at any moment," says Kyle.

The crowd parts nearby. A flash of silver appears as the wheelable ladder I was using earlier comes careening toward us. I push Kyle safely out of the way. My eyes widen when I realize a woman is pushing this ladder through the store like a plow driver to carve a path to the checkouts. *"Ma'am!"*

A man bumps against me and growls, "Watch it, buddy!"

Before I can say anything, he shoves me backward, ready

to hit me until another man stumbles across his path and draws his attention. Only then do I look around to find people yelling, pushing, and shoving. The hairs on my neck stand on end as invisible lightning seems to flicker through the store.

Kyle hurries to my side and says, "What's going on?! Has everyone lost their mind?"

We have to dart aside to avoid getting sucked into a melee. Just to our right, a ten-year-old kid bites a woman's arm.

Lara hops off the toy aisle and onto my shoulders, but I don't bother telling her to stay hidden. "Whoa! *Horsemen!*" she hisses.

"They're *all* horsemen?"

My Hell Sniffer *isn't* glowing.

"No, no, no," Lara mutters. "These folks are all human! But I think they've been affected by a horseman's power! Like, it's put them all into some kind of berserker mode."

Kyle and I duck into the freezer section, where we have space to avoid shoppers.

Kyle says, "There's too much chaos. It's the perfect cover."

"But how could a horseman have infected them all?" I ask Lara.

"They would've needed to physically touch all these people."

A fight spills into the freezer aisle, and before long, people here are whacking each other with frozen food—fish fingers and calamari are flying everywhere. Kyle and I barely make it safely to the garden section. Forget the apocalypse. How will we survive *this*?

"Stop! Stop! Stop!" a familiar voice yells. "Why are you doing this to me?!"

To our right, we see *Pete* huddling in a corner as an old woman tries to bludgeon him with her walker. I rush over, put my box down in order to grab the walker away from her, and toss it aside. The woman stares hard at me, screams in anger, and then rushes after her walker.

"Pete?!" Kyle and I mutter.

We help him up before anyone else can try to beat him to death. "The photo booth!" Kyle calls out. "It's our best bet." We make a beeline to the front. On the way, a man tries to grab Kyle's flamethrower, but she doesn't slow down. Nope. She just swings her elbow at his Adam's apple and leaves him writhing on the floor, clutching his throat.

I have never been more in love.

We throw ourselves into the booth, slide the velvet curtain closed, then hold our breaths as we peer through the gap.

My gaze goes to Pete, who is still shaking. He's lost his Chipmunk feet and cowl, and his green onesie body is stained with grime. "How did—?!" I start to ask. "We thought we'd never see you again!"

Pete tells us he was being transported to a VC facility when "a monster shaped like a sliced avocado *slammed* into the van. It just split it right open." He shows us scratches all over his arms. "But I got out . . . and . . . man, it's crazy out there on the street! Demons are everywhere, dudes!"

Kyle and I peer out into the store as people keep fighting.

Lara climbs onto Pete's lap and says, "It's not exactly a slumber party in here either."

Pete pats her on the head. "I know. But I'm here to help."

"We could use an extra set of eyes to help ID horsemen," I tell him, but before I can say more, I notice that my hands are empty. "Crap! I left the box with the Hell Sniffer outside!" My gaze goes to the space beyond, and it's nowhere to be seen. "*Shit!*"

Before I can think of heading out, Kyle says, "No! We can't just barge out now, Jas. We'll be trampled." She looks at all of us. "First things first. We can't do anything until we get the shoppers under control. Ideas?"

"We need to shock them," says Lara. "Physically. Just totally shock them."

Kyle thinks about it and asks, "What about a cold shower?"

"Cold water?" says Lara, shrugging. "One hundred and twenty volts to their nuts would be better, but sure, maybe cold water could work."

I realize Kyle is peering out of the booth at the ceiling.

"The sprinklers?" I realize. "We can set those off easy."

"Good. While you're doing that, I'll go to the mart's mini VC office and see if the CCTV cams can show us *who* touched all these people." Kyle looks to Pete. "Once people calm down, can you scan the store for anyone acting abnormal?"

Pete nods. "Sure. Once more into the fire, right?" But his hands are clenched tightly around the velvet curtain edge.

"Take Lara with you," I tell him as I hand him the cat.

Kyle holds out a hand, and the rest of us place a palm atop hers.

"Let's do this," I tell them. "Hashtag TeamDoomie!"

We split off in our different directions. I rush to the far right, ducking to avoid a folding chair that someone's thrown into the crowd for whatever reason, and find myself in front of a wall-mounted box that holds the sprinkler controls.

I punch the glass window of the sprinkler box and yank down the pull tab.

Klaxons fill the air. I stumble away as the sprinklers bloom jets of water. Cold showers rain down on everyone. Shoppers stop brawling and stare up at the ceiling. The evil energy of this place almost instantly evaporates. People lower their fists and Saran Wrap roll batons and look like they've just awoken after sleepwalking.

I rush toward the back room, ready to rendezvous with Kyle in the mini VC office, but as I move beyond the checkouts, I spot Gully clenching a pool noodle, gritting his teeth. He looks set to murder whoever fucked his chances at nabbing that bonus. Except it dawns on me that he's not looking at all the soggy products and packaging, but rather, the folks who've calmed down.

"What a waste of time and *energy*," he mutters.

A chill passes over me.

Gully's a fucking horseman.

He catches sight of me and flinches. Somehow, I sense

he knows he's been made.

"Gully! He's one of the four!" I shout as Gully darts off into the crowd behind him.

I race into the back room's mini VC office. Kyle is standing alone next to a bank of cameras.

"*I've got one!*"

"Who?" she asks.

"Gully."

Kyle blinks in surprise but doesn't comment. "Well, look at this," she tells me, pointing at a freeze-framed CCTV image from sometime earlier: Lieutenant Shiner standing at the mart entrance, his palm outstretched to shake everyone's hand. "He touched everyone. He's a fucking horseman too."

"What do we do now?"

Kyle says, "I lost sight of Shiner in the crowd. But he's obviously still here. These are the live feeds." She gestures at the monitors, and we start scanning for our two suspects. "He's gotta be somewhere—"

"*Freeze*," a voice whispers from the shadows.

Abruptly Kyle stops in place as though someone hit *PAUSE* on a video of her. I turn and see Gully standing behind Kyle, his hand on the back of her neck.

Before I can react, Gully places a hand on my shoulder, and a pulse of lightning rushes through me as he says to me, "*Freeze!*"

I'm powerless to fight his command.

21

The Question

Gully studies me closely, a finger pressed against my forehead. I can't move or speak or even *blink*. All I can do is stare ahead as his expression melts into a smirk.

"I don't recall assigning you here," he says.

Footsteps appear as someone else enters. Lieutenant Shiner. He drags Pete by the arm and chucks him over into the shadows nearby. Shiner gets right up in my face and pulls off his eye patch to reveal a left eye with bloodstained whites, and then without warning he punches me, full roundhouse, right in my left eye. Still frozen, I feel nothing. Not the impact, not the rush of blood to my head, not even the hard tiles as I crash to the floor. All I can do is stare at the ceiling as Gully and Shiner stand over me.

Shiner places a booted foot on my chest, then sighs. "Well, well . . . this is anticlimactic." He turns to look at Gully and says, "You fuckin' overdid the paralysis."

Gully steps back, then lifts me up by my collar and chucks me down onto a seat. Shiner has Kyle in a chair facing mine.

"I didn't want to take any chances," Gully says. "Not given what we've learned about them." Out of the corner of my eye, I see Pete get up and shuffle over to Gully. I shift my eyes to try to look at him, but he won't meet my gaze.

He's . . . one of them?!

"Pete," I manage to croak weakly. "But . . . ! We *know you*. . . ."

Shiner cracks his knuckles. "*Hah*. Know him? You never knew any of us."

"But maybe they should," says Gully. "They *should* know who we are, at last."

Shiner walks over to me. He holds his hands to his chest and connects them into an O shape that gives off a feeling made of . . . rage, anger, gleeful malice. An emotional Molotov cocktail that hits me full on—and *burns*. I scream in my head.

All the while Shiner says, "*This* is who I am." But before I think I'll lose my mind, he lowers his hands and the feeling vanishes.

Shiner turns to face Kyle, seemingly ready to share his energy with her.

"Get away from her!" I yell, but my words barely escape in a slur.

Gully blocks my view, creates an O shape with his hands, and shares his own abyssal identity. It's the same retail overlord energy that Gully always radiates whenever he's controlling people with mindless bullshit work—except now it's maxed up to *1,000 percent*.

Gully goes over to Kyle. But Shiner pushes Pete toward me and says to him, "Your turn." When Pete wavers, Shiner grabs the back of his neck, fingers digging into his skin.

"Don't be shy around your new friends," Shiner growls. "*Show them.*"

Pete forms an O shape and shares his abyssal energy. With a zing, I find my brain inundated with images of brightly colored clothing, Amazon delivery boxes, and online sales listings for shoes and hats and jackets. I feel this *hunger* to buy, collect, wear, own, and buy some more.

Pete pulls away to gush out, "I'm sorry, sorry, sorry, *sorry*! I wish I didn't have to screw you guys over . . . but I . . . I . . . can't abandon my mission." He looks away. "In the abyss we never had real things . . . and now that I'm here, I *have* to see this mission through, so I can have first dibs on mountains of amazing stuff left behind by humans."

Pete finally turns to look at me.

But Shiner just shoves him backward and then says to Kyle and me, "So. Now you know *who* is inside these bodies."

"If I had to do it again, I'd've chosen someone younger," Gully muses as he peers down at himself.

"But in order to conserve energy for our mission, our incarnations had to be efficient. We needed dead bodies of people who matched our *exact* individual emotions," says Shiner. "And they had to be *freshly* dead."

"So we waited, and waited, and *waited*," says Gully. "Floated unseen for weeks, watching people, until one by one, we found compatible humans on the verge of death. We then swooped in *just* as they died."

The two horsemen study me with an eerie calm.

I finally manage to swallow, and I mutter: "We . . . will . . . stop you."

Neither of them seem to have heard me. Shiner just smiles faintly and says, "As we said, we slipped in just as they died. However, things didn't go exactly according to plan for one of us."

"You'll . . . never . . ."

I want to say, *You'll never win. We'll fight you!* But Shiner's last sentence is echoing in my head, and I realize there's only three horsemen here.

"You're starting to ask the sixty-four-thousand-dollar question, right?" says Gully.

Where's the last horseman?

Shiner pulls something out of his pocket. The Hell Sniffer. He turns it on and aims the flashlight at himself, then Gully, then Pete, all the while causing the device to glow. Finally, he aims it at the ground, and it darkens. "Behold," he whispers before at last pointing it at *me*.

Light blinds me.

"What . . . no . . . I . . ."

No, not possible. This has to be a joke. A meaningless, sick fucking joke. But my breathing becomes difficult as a strange, invisible weight gathers around my shoulders and chest, squeezing tight.

"The fourth host was seventeen," Shiner explains, chucking aside the flashlight. "Some kid who was lost in unbearable despair and wandering through life in a daze. A kid who had an accident right *here*, in this mart."

My accident in aisle three?

"That young man became the host for an entity your kind would call . . . *hopelessness*," says Shiner. "An entity who should've been the most powerful of our quartet."

"No!" I hiss, averting my gaze to Kyle, who is fighting through her paralysis to shake her head. I squeeze my eyes shut. "No! I'm not a part of your mission!"

"Well, you're half-right," says Shiner. "Here's what happened: Hopelessness found you when you were dying in the hospital, sank into you, and was ready to incarnate inside your soon-to-be-dead body. But then, somehow, you survived . . . and actually trapped him inside you."

Gully shakes his head. "It's fuckin' unbelievable. You can barely arrange an endcap properly, but somehow your weak-ass body contained a *horseman*."

My gaze seeks out Pete, praying that he'll somehow contradict the others. But he just stares at his feet as he mumbles, "Hopelessness can't escape from wherever he is, in you."

"But no matter," says Shiner. "For some time now, we've been carefully engineering events all around you . . . to help free our fellow horseman and let him gain control."

My gaze goes back to Kyle to see tears streaming down her cheeks. "I won't let him take over my body . . . I won't let him win. . . ."

"Ah, but we haven't even started," says Gully.

Gully wanders over to Kyle and runs a hand through her yellow hair. I yell out for him to leave her alone, but he just chuckles softly, then heads back to me.

"Easy," he whispers in a strangely tender voice. "You wanted to see your past? Well, humankind's darkest memories live on inside the abyss . . . so let me share something of *yours* that we saved."

Gully creates another O shape with his hands, and out of it flows an energy that pierces through my skull and makes my vision go dark. . . .

22

The Living Room

I see a picture of Kyle and me sitting in my parents' living room. It's late at night and the only glow comes from a TV that neither of us is watching. Kyle is sitting cross-legged on one end of the couch, her back to me, while I'm hunched forward on the other end, staring at my hands.

Suddenly, I'm *in* the memory, looking out through the eyes of my earlier self. I realize I'm not staring at my hands but rather a brochure that reads, *Vanguard Thanks You for Enlisting.* Underneath is some smaller text that mentions "orientation day" for new recruits.

I'm confused. I want to inspect the brochure closer, but I can't move.

I cannot do anything, except let the memory play out.

My former self turns to face Kyle's back and says in a strangled tone, "I . . . thought you were only *thinking* about enlisting?" I shake my head. "When were you gonna tell me you *already* enlisted?"

I can feel my heartbeat rushing.

"I don't need your permission," she mutters, standing and facing a window. "It's my life."

"That you'll be throwing away!" I call out. "Geez! Do you have a death wish? You could get mauled by a demon!"

"I can get mauled by a demon while waiting at Starbucks. Look, I can't have this discussion again," she tells me, beginning to walk away.

I stand up and try to grab her arm. "No. Listen!"

Kyle spins around fast, the motion flinging me back a step and releasing her from my grip. "All I ever do is listen to you!" she snaps before looking away. "All I ever do is listen to how Vanguard is bullshit and corrupt and not fixing the world in any real way. But you know what? We wouldn't still *be here* if it wasn't for them. Which you'd remember if you actually stopped mainlining conspiracy theories!"

"This isn't about me," I tell her. "This is—"

Kyle shakes her head, gaze lowered. "No. It's about *me*." Her arms are wrapped around herself, her hands clutching at her sleeves to twist the fabric. "I don't wanna be afraid of *everything*. That's why I joined VC: to do *something*." She exhales sharply. "I can't keep doing nothing with you."

"Fine," I breathe, holding my hands out. "Let's not talk about this anymore tonight."

A stillness passes over her before she mumbles, "I'm not just talking about VC." Her eyes finally meet mine. "I can't keep going around in circles with you . . . I can't keep . . . I . . . don't want us to—" She stumbles for words, gestures at the space between her and me. "I don't want us to be an *us* anymore."

"You want to . . ."

You want to break up?

I think that's what I was going to say, back then. But my earlier self pivots to ask, "What do you want us to be, then? Strangers who never even met?"

The silence pushes down on me, hard.

"Kyle," I plead, "you and I, we're—"

"We're just—" She looks away before her voice gets so soft that I don't even know if she's talking to me. But her whisper cuts right through me: "We're only ever going to just . . . fall apart."

Suddenly I think I remember what was going on in my head, back in that moment. For weeks I'd been terrified that Kyle would enlist in VC and get killed by a demon. But standing there in the living room back then, I finally realized: *I've already lost her. She's already gone. . . .*

The memory skips ahead to something else.

A few weeks after our breakup, I was wandering through the aisles of the mart in a state of nothingness, a zombie in a work vest. I could barely take in anything clearly. It was sometime in the middle of another endless shift when I heard a creaking from overhead. I looked up to see a dangling overhead decoration of a piggy bank, swinging unevenly.

I watched as it started to fall. But I couldn't move out of

the way, not quickly enough.

Or maybe I didn't want to.

The memories melt away, and I'm back in the VC office.

Kyle starts to call out to me, "I'm sorry" over and over. I can hear her crying, but she won't look at me, and soon I don't have the strength to look at her.

Shiner crouches beside me and says, "After you left the hospital, my companions wanted to show you *that* memory. They thought it would break you. But I convinced them that your devastating breakup would've seemed meaningless without happy memories of Kyle." He grabs my chin and gets me to look squarely at Kyle. "So we needed you to reconnect and fall in love all over again. We needed you to believe you had something beautiful to lose . . . before we could show you the truth." His voice becomes a whisper: "The truth that it's all hopeless with her anyway—always has been, always will be."

My thoughts go to what Kyle told me last night. The reason why she didn't tell me about *us* when she learned about my amnesia: *I felt that we were just doomed to fall apart.* I remember how she quickly clarified that statement with the words, *Because of Hell Portal Day and the chaos . . .*

Now I realize that second part was a lie.

My eyes meet hers, and I whisper, "You . . . never believed we'd make things work, did you? *That's* the reason why you didn't tell me the truth. You thought our relationship was doomed because of *us*."

And maybe she was right all along.

"Jasper . . . ," she begins.

A chill swells inside my chest, radiating outward to fill me with a crippling numbness. The room just falls away, or rather, *I* just fall through everything around me, and into a hole inside my mind.

I let myself tumble. . . .

The Void

Time skews. But eventually I realize I've somehow landed on solid ground. I'm sprawled on my back, but I can't feel the surface below me. It takes all my strength, but I rise to a crouch. I can't see anything beyond my own hands; everything around me is a cocoon of darkness. Am I in the abyss? Or is this some part of the abyss that lives inside *me*?

I don't know. It's like being a million miles away from reality.

All I can hear is the sound of my breathing getting faster and louder as I feel myself starting to panic. But then another sound cuts through the void. *Kyle.* Her voice is distant, muffled, but I can hear her crying as she tries to apologize to me. I only manage to hear three words clearly: *I was . . . afraid . . .*

Through all the confusion, all the numbness, I somehow find myself thinking back to something Kyle said in the ISO: *I was afraid to let myself hope for anything.* And as I dwell on those words, I finally realize that *this* is why she didn't reveal our past to me sooner.

But she *wanted* to believe in us.

This is the real reason. Deep down I just know it.

"Come on," I whisper to myself, again and again, until I start rising to my feet.

Get back to her, Jasper. Come on!

I stumble forward in search of an escape, but only manage a dozen yards before I crash against a barrier made of more darkness. Some sort of wall made of impenetrable, invisible bricks. "It's not real," I whisper, but my hands can't break through whatever it is.

Abruptly, my gaze catches sight of a glimmer that flickers through a tiny hole in the barrier. I hurry over and press my face to the hole. Through it I see a glimpse of the mart's VC office. Which must be the view through my *actual* eyes, as the abyssal of Hopelessness controls my body and looks around. At last, he focuses on Kyle.

The abyssal uses *my* body to walk closer to her. "Hello there," he says with my voice. "I too have a specific power. Would you care to experience it?"

Kyle flinches when my hands touch her shoulders. A glimmering light flickers around my fingers as Hopelessness channels his abyssal power *into* Kyle.

"Stop!" I yell out, but the sound doesn't leave the void.

A switch seems to go off in Kyle as her eyes glaze over.

Through me, Hopelessness whispers in her ear: "There's a place I know where judgments melt away and people stop fighting. A place where people surrender to their pain, their fears, their fates. A place where nothing matters. A place that is but a feeling."

Kyle rocks back into her seat.

"You see it now, don't you?" he asks her. "You see the truth—"

"That there's no point in fighting," Kyle whispers. "There's no point in anything."

He reaches out to cup her cheek, and she stares right through me. Her gaze holds nothing, empty and deadened.

"No!" I scream into the void.

The hole in the barrier seals up, and I'm plunged back into darkness.

My thoughts are a spinning haze. Distant muffled voices from the real world make it hard to think. The horsemen are talking among themselves. Gully and Shiner greet Hopelessness with a cheer and talk about what a pain in the ass it was to reunite the four of them.

Shiner says, "Why are you still sharing a body with this human? You will never actually incarnate if you do not find a suitable empty shell or empty out this current one."

Hopelessness says in my voice, "I have the human contained, all under control. Let us not waste any more time."

"Fine, then," says Gully. "Let's begin."

I know I need to get out of this void. ASAP.

My attention shifts from the horsemen and over to the space around me. I begin trying to take in deep breaths and center myself, until something flickers in my periphery. I turn to see a faint light embedded in the ground beside me. I kneel down, touch black sand, and brush this away to uncover a marble of swirling colors.

"What the—"

Unearthing the marble causes a scene to play in my mind: I'm sitting on the stoop outside my folks' apartment building and an orange cat is climbing onto my feet. It's the stray that would always hang out with me when I was a kid. This! It's . . . a memory! That I'm now *re-remembering*.

My gaze sweeps over the ground, and I notice dozens more glowing marbles buried in the sand. Just by focusing my attention on the marbles, sand rolls away from them, and the memories rush back.

I remember my dad teaching me how to ride a bike by daring me to run over his shoes, which I actually do, at least *three* times. . . . I remember a roller-coaster ride where I went so fast that my screams couldn't catch up with my ears. . . . I remember a double rainbow above Sundown City Park. . . . There's the scrunchy noise of birthday-present wrapping paper coming undone. . . . The laughter of my grandmother as I try to take a picture of her . . .

It's my life in moments.

A marble a few steps away catches my eye. It's grayer than the others, but something about it screams out silently to me: *Remember!* So I reach out to touch it, and my mind is sucked backward in time to reexperience—

Blackness. My eyes won't open.

I'm neither asleep nor unconscious but seem to be *trapped* in my body. I hear distant voices, PA chimes, the beeping from a machine. The smell of disinfectant stabs my nose. *Am I in a hospital?* I ask myself, but thinking gets hard when I become aware of an incredible pulsing pain. *Was I in an accident? Think, Jasper! The last thing that happened . . . something . . . fell on me . . . from the mart ceiling . . .*

I try to escape the pain . . .

And I find refuge in a corner of my mind, where instead of pain there's just a numbing tiredness. A weariness that makes me think I've been fighting too hard, too long, too much, that I'm torturing myself by always keeping my head above water. This tiredness . . . It practically speaks to me and tells me to *let go.* Tells me to let the pain carry me away into nothingness.

So I dive into the deepest swell of pain.

It burns but carries me.

But then I feel someone take my hand and I recognize the touch: Kyle. She's sitting next to me, and I force myself to get out of the deepest pain so I can listen to her say, "Jasper. Please don't leave me. *Please . . .*"

Kyle wraps her arms around my motionless body, her touch goes into me, and the sharp edges of all the pain soften a little. She says—

"I'm sorry. I didn't mean all those terrible things I said that night. I . . . felt I was drowning in your fear and despair . . . and it reminded me too much of my own hopelessness. All the shit I couldn't deal with. All the fear I tried to block out." Kyle's voice gets softer. "I didn't want to think or feel anything. That's why I pushed you away.

"When I said we were doomed to fall apart . . . I . . . didn't mean because of *us*." Kyle lets out a wavering breath before she whispers, "Sometimes I feel like there's this dark pit inside *me* that poisons everything, and I don't know how to get rid of it." She squeezes my hand and doesn't speak for a long moment. "I don't know how to fix anything . . . but there's one thing I truly know. *I love you*."

Sounds of other people emerge. A doctor and nurses.

They try to usher Kyle out to let me rest.

No . . . stay . . . !

"I love you, Jasper." She kisses me on the cheek. "So you better get the fuck out of that coma and come back. *Do. Not. Give. Up.*"

Kyle leaves the room. An immense pain washes over me again, but this time, every fiber of my being is telling me to hold on. And I make a vow to stay and fight. But just like that, my numbing tiredness makes a return, and this time, it feels less like an emotion from within me, and more like something from *outside* me. What I think might be a . . . *creature.*

Finally revealed, the creature stretches out inside my mind and speaks to me in a low voice: *It is pointless with her. . . . You will never make things work with her. . . . You know this. . . .*

Who are you? I ask the creature.

Let me help you drift away, he tells me. *You were so close earlier. . . .*

He tries to push me toward the greatest swells of pain.

But I think of what Kyle said to me, and a lightness emerges inside me and spreads outward. A warmth that causes the creature to retreat a little. Suddenly, I get this deep sense that maybe I can overpower him, so I channel my feelings *onto* his invisible body and force him into a corner of my mind. I trap him.

Let me go! the creature hisses.

When I refuse, he wavers before saying, *So be it. Hope is easily forgotten. How will you fight to survive your injuries . . . if you do not remember* why *you wish to remain?*

And just like that, everything goes blank.

I leave the memory and realizations click.

The abyssal thought I would lose all willpower to fight if he erased my memories. He thought I would die and become an empty vessel for his incarnation. But somehow, even without memories, the hope that Kyle inspired couldn't be destroyed. That hope—it helped me to fight my injuries and allowed me to keep on imprisoning the abyssal within my subconscious.

"*Hope*," I whisper into the void.

I move closer to the barrier that traps me in the void. Using my imagination, I pretend that the barrier is a movie screen. I project upon it a supercut of what Kyle and I have experienced over the last few days. I see our adventures in HD widescreen color, and the chill of the void starts to melt away.

I hear a rumbling, as though the barrier's invisible bricks

are cracking. At the same time, a faceless wraith materializes to my right. Hopelessness, in his true form. He's turned his attention away from the real world in order to face me in the void.

Quickly I shift my supercut of memories onto *him*.

Hopelessness flinches as images ripple around and *through* his ghostly body. He steps toward me, arms outstretched and ready to attack, and whispers, *You know deep down . . . that you cannot kill me.* His voice breaks into a soft laugh. *You could not do so all those months ago, and you will not do so right here . . . now that I know you better than ever.*

My projected images flicker.

He's right. I was only able to trap him earlier.

"Fine. I'll settle for that again," I whisper.

Hopelessness begins to charge toward me. But while he knows me better than before, I know now, more clearly than ever, why I'm fighting. I focus on the memories of Kyle and all the feelings embedded inside them. I open myself up to the joy, the magic, the connection, the sheer sense of *not-alone-anymore*–ness . . .

My feelings rush outward, and the void erupts into a shimmering haze of starlight that swirls and arcs everywhere. My gaze shifts to the space in front of me, just as Hopelessness sinks to his knees and becomes a blur buried behind the lights. I hear him roar.

Once more, he is a prisoner.

24

Swarm

With a gasp I open my eyes. I take in the dimness of the mart back room, and every fiber of my being cries out, *I'm back! I'm back!* I suck in *actual* air and shudder. But instantly I freeze when I take in my surroundings—I'm standing in a circle with the horsemen, each of us a dozen feet apart, to echo points on a compass. Their eyes are closed. But shimmering cords of energy are rushing out from their feet and flowing in the direction of aisle nine.

They're expanding the portal.

How do I stop them?

The room is quivering faintly, the air bristling with current, and for a flash of a moment, it all seems as though everything could be hopeless. At least, until I realize that this feeling is coming from the depths of my subconsciousness. Specifically, from the abyssal of Hopelessness.

"*No,*" I breathe softly. "*You* cannot stop me."

This is my last chance to defeat them. I reach into my pocket for the gun that is still where I left it. As I pull it out,

I see a flutter of motion in front of me as Pete opens his eyes and startles.

Shit!

Pete lowers his gaze, and I realize I'm pointing a barrel at him. Logic tells me I need to take him out—*pull the trigger*—but my head fills with an image of Kyle, Pete, and me dressed up like Chipmunks. I think of how we laughed so hard. And I lower my weapon.

Pete, I mouth. *It's not too late.*

Pete wavers, then slowly takes a couple of steps backward. His abyssal energy stops flowing out to the portal. He mouths the word *hurry* and darts off quietly into the shadows. Just like that, I sense that the portal is nearly finished expanding.

I've got to stop the other horsemen.

I've got to *kill them*.

I raise my gun to Lieutenant Shiner. My finger rests on the trigger, and I freeze for one heartbeat, then another, until Shiner's eyes flutter open. Instantly, I know I have no choice anymore. I squeeze the trigger and the air fills with a *pop* as a bullet goes into his chest. Shiner crumples to the ground and I see blood pooling out fast from his side.

Quickly I spin around, raising my weapon at Gully.

But in that same motion, Gully opens his eyes and lunges to grab my arm. Energy pulses into my body as he yells out, "Freeze! I command you to stop!"

My body goes limp. Suddenly all I can do is sway and

stare into Gully's face as he grabs my gun and throws it aside.

Gully catches sight of Shiner, then yells out sharply and headbutts me. Suddenly I'm on the floor. Gully straddles me and tries to choke me out. My vision fills with a sudden constellation of gray stars. I can't feel anything, can't breathe.

Out of nowhere, a blur of white rushes over and slams into his head. Gully lets go of me. Tumbles to the side. It takes all my energy, but I manage to turn my head to the side, and that's when I see Lara zinging around him. Gully grabs at thin air, until finally snagging her tail. Lara shrieks as he flings her to the floor. He raises a foot, ready to stomp on her.

Then he pauses.

My gaze shifts to take in Pete standing behind Gully, his hand pressed to the back of Gully's neck. Abruptly Pete commands, "Okay! It's time for a makeover! I want you to *want* to try on . . ." He points at a partially opened box of off-brand T-shirts. "*Those!*"

Gully tries to turn around and strike Pete, but soon he's unable to fight a compulsion to stagger over to the T-shirts. He grabs a small canary-yellow shirt. Barely manages to pull it over his body. He looks like a vacuum-packed piece of meat. "Enough!" Gully says in a choke. "Stop!"

Pete simply touches his shoulder and says, "More!"

On and on, Gully puts on four more shirts in a matter of seconds. Pete is sweating profusely, and I sense that his power is going to fade soon. I need to help him. *Now.*

With Gully focused on the clothes, I feel my paralysis begin to weaken. I force myself to stagger to my feet. My limbs are shaky as hell, and I don't have the strength to physically strike him. But I catch sight of a box of women's athletic wear.

Supertight spandex garments.

I knock the box over and kick the items toward Gully. "Pete!" I call out.

Pete sees them and commands Gully, "Put them *all* on!"

"Do it! Do it!" Lara yells out as well.

Gully pales but shakily puts on a tiny spandex top, which gets stuck over his head, clinging tightly to his face and neck. His hands keep moving on their own, to add a second, then third layer, until Gully crashes down in a writhing heap. He struggles for air, until finally his huge limbs thud down at his sides.

The air shimmers as his abyssal spirit rises out of his body. And dissolves. My paralysis fully melts away and pain floods over my body. I collapse to my knees. But just as Pete helps me to my feet, asking me if I'm okay, the overhead lights flicker off.

"What happened?" Lara calls out.

My eyes adjust to the dimness, and I stare at the ground to realize Shiner's body has vanished, replaced instead by a trail of blood that leads off into the shadows. My pulse is racing harder than ever. I'm about to call out to the others, until I realize everything has gone deathly silent. "Guys?" I hiss to Lara and Pete.

Motion ripples to the right, and I flinch when I see Lara running around in circles, trying to chase her tail. "Jasper!

I . . . can't . . . I . . ." Lara struggles to speak as she fights like hell against *herself*. And just to her right, Pete is an equally insane sight as his left hand tries to stop his right from punching his face.

Shiner's berserker power.

I step backward, only to bump into a hard shape, and spin around to see the lieutenant. Shiner grabs me by the collar and hurls me through the air. My back crashes against a wall, and I crumple to my knees. I look up just as he holds a hand over my forehead, ready to possess me.

I flinch. But he pulls back and laughs.

"People don't feel anything when I use my power," he mutters, gesturing at Pete and Lara, before smirking faintly. "But I'm not gonna use my energy on you. I want you to feel *everything*."

I rise up and try to flee. But Shiner lunges forward and sends me slamming back against the wall. He pulls out two daggers and pins the sides of my shirt and vest to the wall. I try to pull free but can't.

Shiner stalks over to a nearby worktable, where he picks up a nail gun that one of the clerks left there. Before I know it, he's a dozen feet in front of me, and he shakes his head as he studies the nail gun. "You know, I'm always shocked at the utter disregard that clerks have for workplace health and safety rules. Retail . . . *man*, it's a fuckin' deathtrap."

Shiner fires a nail into his own palm. Takes in the blood and laughs. Doesn't seem to feel a thing. Then his eyes line up with mine and he says, "We have already greatly expanded the portal. It will not take much for me to finish it off. But first . . ."

Shiner steps closer to me, aims the gun at my head, and I see a silver spike in the gun's barrel. I turn away, but in doing so, I spot a dark shape on the ground a dozen feet away.

My gun.

Everything slows down as I pull away from the wall. My clothes rip free of the daggers. I throw myself toward the gun. Land on my belly. Grab the weapon. Spin around just as Shiner fires off a nail.

Metal grazes past my cheek as I lift the weapon and fire— over and over and over.

I keep punching holes in the dark.

Then finally, I hear a sudden thud as Shiner collapses to the floor, and I hold my breath until I see a shimmer of light escape his body.

I get to my feet and stumble toward the center of the room where Pete and Lara shake themselves out of their mania. They rush over and ask if I'm okay. But I just call out, "What's happening out in the store? Is the portal already wide enough?" My next question crashes into the others: "And where's Kyle?"

We rush out of the back room and into the store. Now that everything is soaked from the sprinklers, most of the shoppers have left, but there are several dozen people still milling about, trying to find a soggy bargain.

"Kyle!" I yell.

Pete shouts at the nearby shoppers to leave, but they just shove past him.

"Jasper—the portal!" Lara calls out, and I see her pointing at aisle nine, where the guards are nowhere to be seen. The gate has been opened, and the portal is glowing bloodred. It's expanded to eight feet tall, which has caused the upper frame of the aisle quarantine to distort.

"It's not wide enough yet!" Pete exclaims. "But . . . it's getting larger! I don't know how—"

Lara interrupts, "There must be someone nearby still powering it. Look!" She points at a thin thread of energy that is running directly into the portal. Feeding it.

I spin around and chase the thread all the way to a crouched person in the next aisle: Kyle. Her shoulders are slumped forward, her head low as she remains lost in a horseman's curse of hopelessness. At her feet, her emotional energy—her hopelessness magnified by her Doomie power—keeps rushing out toward the portal. She's making the portal wider.

"We have to stop her!" Pete calls out. "Quickly, before the other abyssals can get through—"

His words are cut short as shapes emerge from the portal. Tendrils. Talons. Wings. Monsters tumble out. The three of us have no time to hesitate as Pete helps me lift Kyle, and we hurry away to seek refuge far beyond aisle one, in a corner next to the dairy space. Lara hops up onto a freezer to stare around, and she calls out, "They're spreading through the store! Shit . . . some are headed this way!"

Pete gives me a look that says, *We need to hurry!*

While he grabs abandoned carts and boxes and tries to form a makeshift barricade, I kneel on the ground, holding Kyle in my arms, and I call out, "Kyle!"

I try to shake her, but her head just lolls back as her eyes soak up the flickering halogen light above us. *She's not even . . . here. Is she?* The ground is shuddering; the aisles themselves are rattling wildly, telling me that we're running out of time.

"Kyle, you need to wake up now! We can stop the abyssals! We can do this! But you need to get up—now."

No response.

"Kyle!"

A nearby scream makes me look up. A dozen yards away, a shrieking old woman is trying to clamber over Pete's barricade, but she gets pulled backward by a human-sized insect. A white parasitic tick. It jabs her spine with a proboscis and immediately begins *sucking* her blood, turning its translucent body dark red.

In mere seconds, the tick chucks her dry body to the floor. The insect barges through the barricade and ambles toward us. I shield Kyle with my body, then look over to see Pete roaring out, "Stop!"

Pete closes his eyes, places his hands on the ground, and casts out shimmering energy across the floor as he says,

"Monster shoppers! You've come to the right place . . . to find a bargain! I want you to *want to* shop till you drop!"

While Pete needed to touch humans to affect them, the demons seem more susceptible as they halt their charge and face the shelves. The white tick grabs a red-sequin caftan and tries putting it on. "Quickly!" Lara calls out to me. "I don't think Pete can spread his power like that for long! He—" She suddenly hops up and down. "Shit! The portal! It's almost completely widened on our side!"

Barely seconds later, the energy leaving Kyle's body finally ebbs, and the portal begins to rumble. A sound that tells me instantly, it's *done*. The abyssals will be here in moments.

We failed.

I hold Kyle closer and plead with her to wake. I can feel her growing cold in my arms. I check her pulse: she's fading away. At the same time, something crumbles in the depths of my mind, and Hopelessness begins to rise up from his prison.

"No," I hiss. "You are *not* taking over my body! Not now!"

I can almost hear him laugh in my ears.

From inside my head, he says to me, *I have no more interest in your body. There is a reason why I chose to stay inside you, despite finally being free—I was merely waiting for my new vessel to be ready.*

The air shimmers as Hopelessness begins drifting out of me and into *Kyle*. I stagger away from her, but his abyssal spirit keeps flowing in her direction, and I hear him whisper,

In a few moments, she will be the perfect hollow vessel . . . for me to finally incarnate within.

He knows she's on the verge of dying.

No. I kneel again to pull Kyle into my arms, and that's when I whisper, "Kyle. I know what it feels like to think you're always gonna fuck things up. To feel like everything is always *hopeless* in this dumpster fire kingdom, and that it'd be easier to let everything go."

My voice hitches in my throat as Hopelessness continues flowing into her body. In a matter of moments, he'll be out of me entirely.

"Kyle, when I hung in the balance, your love reminded me not to give up. I held on because of *you*. And . . . I love you too." I kiss her on the forehead. Hold her tighter. "Come back, Kyle. Not to the worst-ever places in this city, but to *our own place*. Our place where we make our own damn rules. Our place where it doesn't matter what's on fire in the city, or what's blowing up, because we've got one another. Come back to *us*."

I feel a pulsing inside me as once more, a lightness floods through my body. I feel it warm my chest, the air, the very space between Kyle and me. Abruptly my energy disrupts Hopelessness. It causes his spirit to stop flowing outward, and the part of him that remains within me is yanked, *hard*, back into the depths of my mind and into that prison.

I whisper to Kyle, "We're not over. Not even close."

Her eyes slowly focus on my face. Her gaze meets mine,

and she takes in a sudden, sharp breath and shudders, reaching out to grab on to me. I hold her tightly and try to stop her shivering.

"My turn to say, 'Welcome back to the world, baby'?" I whisper.

"You're *you*?" she whispers into my shoulder.

"We both are . . . us."

And something more. I hear a roar from the depths of my mind as Hopelessness rails within his prison, but he seems to be a smaller presence than before. Looking over at Kyle, I think I know why: Hopelessness has been split into two halves—one trapped in me and the other in *her*.

Kyle flinches as she too seems to sense this, but I keep holding her tightly and say, "You can keep him locked inside a corner of your mind. Use your hope, your joy . . . to make a prison. You got this."

Kyle takes in a deep breath and calms.

"He's . . . weakened. I'm holding him back, I think," she explains.

"Good." We get to our feet to discover that the abyssals have yet to emerge, and I call out, "It's not over yet! We can still close the portal! We just need the right energy."

"It's . . . just us against hell?" Kyle whispers. "Do we have enough power?"

I dare not answer that.

"We'll need to get closer to the portal, then."

But how? Pete's power is waning. Monsters are starting

to take notice of us. The tick is heading our way—and it's found a red cowboy hat to match its caftan.

Kyle and I swap a look, and my mind goes blank.

Then Lara yells, "*Vanguard!*"

Over in the distance, glass shatters as Vanguardians shoot the locked doors. Seconds later they march into the mart, and the monsters instantly shift their attention to the massing soldiers.

"Now!" says Kyle.

She leads me through the space behind the aisles, and our bodies line up with aisle nine, where monsters have now stopped emerging. The portal is larger than ever. Abyssal silhouettes have started filling up the circular shape, darkening the red glow as their ghostly limbs and claws try to pierce through the portal skin. They'll only need moments to break through.

I turn to face Kyle and hold tightly to her hands. I gaze into her eyes and whisper, "We can do this. We can use our hope to light up this darkness."

Kyle closes her eyes and so do I.

In my thoughts, I think of my fantasy of Kyle and me driving off into the desert in that VW van. But this time I see myself *in* that vision. I feel myself leaning forward in that driver's seat. I hear Kyle laugh as we roll into the distance, the future, the world we've yet to make.

All that I'm feeling rushes out of my chest to flood out all around me. My eyes flutter open, and I see the abyssals writhe and hiss within the portal. The hell hole buckles violently. It twists into a swirling, jagged silhouette, then a wild blur, then finally . . .

A shockwave explodes out of aisle nine, throwing Kyle and me backward, and we slam against the freezer doors. Bulbs shatter; shelves collapse. We hold tightly to one another as the whole world seems to buckle underneath us. Then, as quickly as the energy struck us, all goes silent.

We stumble to our knees to stare into aisle nine . . . at nothing. We gaze around to see demons now motionless on the spot, stunned by the shockwave, and lit only by the flickering emergency lights; their grotesque bodies might as well be melted, distorted mannequins.

Then the stillness breaks. Vanguard soldiers charge forward in a wave of Kevlar and steel, and their rifle shots and flamethrower fire turn the aisles golden. First, the space at the checkouts clears, followed by the aisles around us, until at last, a lone soldier guides us through the ruins and out to the street.

Into the light.

Gates of Hell

Without AC, we travel with the windows rolled down, and the desert air turns our van into a mobile rotisserie. But none of us complains. Not Lara, who is curled up on the dashboard in a puddle of yellow light. Not Kyle, who drives us onward, her hair now dyed sky blue.

She smiles and says, "I think we're almost there."

Up ahead, a small convoy of cars and RVs is headed in a straight line through the desert nothingness. I'm about to crane forward until something falls into my lap. A Polaroid photo of Kyle, Lara, and me. I reach up to stick it back on the ceiling above, where dozens of other photos have been taped to the felt lining.

What I see are photographs of all our visits to best worst places. Our trips to ghost towns damaged by Hell Portal Day. Our journey to an illegal underground museum full of monster remains. It's been six months since Black Friday, and we've seen more fucked-up weird shit than we could ever have imagined.

But today could be something else.

A crunch draws my attention as we roll over the remains of a Vanguard mesh barricade. Lara stirs and says, "Huh? We there yet?"

"Almost," I reply.

I look around to see what must have once been an enormous Vanguard fence. The guard station is abandoned.

"Look!" I call out, pointing to my right at where a quarantine zone stands empty. "That would've been where a portal once stood."

In the months since Black Friday, VC never found out what happened at the mart, since all the CCTV cams were fried. The store was permanently closed under the excuse of a salmonella outbreak. But Kyle and I refused to let everything stay hidden. We anonymously uploaded the Vanguard research video on portal closure to WikiLeaks. And people have started to close portals everywhere. No one knows how many have been shut, but it's happening. The world is healing.

But for now, that's a job we're letting other folks handle.

Kyle parks our van near some other vehicles. We step outside into the hot-hot air, and Lara plays dead under my arm. Only then do we spot Pete and Edwin waiting nearby, leaning against an old sedan. The pair see us and hurry over.

"Hey, guys!" says Kyle and Lara.

"About time!" says Pete.

Pete is wearing jeans and a T-shirt that reads, *I*

SURVIVED BLACK FRIDAY AND ALL I GOT WAS THIS DUMB T-SHIRT—the same thing he's worn for weeks now. These days, his only prized accessory is a Polaroid camera that hangs on a chest strap that he's used to document our adventures.

"We thought you'd gotten lost," says Edwin, with a wide smile that still looks weird on his stern face.

I'm about to greet them, but my attention is distracted by a distant crater . . . of fire. "Whoa!" I gasp. "So there it is! The natural gas field."

Edwin nods. "Yep."

On Hell Portal Day, a fire demon apparently broke a hole in the ground here and ignited the gases below. VC could not extinguish the flames, so they just walled it up and let it burn. But now that Vanguard has abandoned this place, that wall has long since come down.

Pete and Edwin rush farther ahead, but Kyle and I waver when we catch sight of a nearby chunk of metal sticking out of the sand. A jagged scrap covered in human blood.

I turn to face Kyle, and she whispers, "We'll never be able to fix everything."

I was actually thinking those *exact* words, and I wonder: Was that sentiment *ours*, or something sparked by the *abyssal* still lurking deep inside us? I don't know.

Even though it's been months, Hopelessness remains trapped deep inside Kyle and me. He's still dangerous, still a shadow on my thoughts, and surely hers too. But I take in a breath and remind myself, *We'll continue to hold him back one day at a time.*

I take Kyle's hand and whisper, "Maybe we'll never be able to fix everything. But that's okay." A smile comes easily to me. "Maybe that's *much* more than okay."

Kyle smiles back and squeezes my hand. We continue to stroll on ahead, and minutes later we reach a huge sign that reads, WELCOME TO THE GATES OF HELL. FIRE-PROOF SUITS ONLY $50. A dozen yards to the left, a makeshift building of scrap wood bears the word *MOTEL*.

Kyle and I chuckle. Until she leans in to kiss me.

We head closer to the Gates of Hell, and only then does my gaze catch sight of something far, far ahead on the horizon—a sliver of turquoise blue. Kyle shifts as she too catches sight of the ocean in the distance.

"We'll get there too," I whisper to her. "We're going to see it all."

And she turns to me and smiles and says, "I hope so."

VC POINTS

VC POINTS
CONVERSION RATE: 20 VC = 1 USD

STREET
Passing a roadblock: 1 VC / $0.05
Passing a VC poster: 1 VC / $0.05
A pedestrian can make a maximum of one dollar a day by walking the streets. Individual posters will only gift a point per day.

RETAIL EXAMPLES
Baskin-Robbins single cone = 60 VC / $3
Subway footlong = 120 VC / $6

COMPENSATION
Points for witnessing violence: 400 VC / $20
Points for getting injured: 2,000 VC / $100
Points for calling in a demon: 10,000 VC / $500
Points for getting affected by brimstone: 200 VC / $10

FINES
Disorderly conduct: 2,000 VC / $100

Acknowledgments

To my agent, Dan Lazar, thank you for taking a chance on a very bizarre early manuscript. I'm startled by the amount of time and effort that you invested in this project long before I was even a client of yours. Whatever guidance I believed an agent could provide, you have certainly exceeded that by miles!

To my editor, Dave Linker, thank you for your belief in this story. I am truly grateful for the way that you've helped me wrangle the wild beast that is *Aisle Nine*. Together we've battled unwieldy early drafts, vanquished plot holes, and slain tons of logistical gremlins. Your insights and wisdom have been awesome.

To the brilliant folks at Writers House, HarperCollins, and HarperCollins Australia, I am most appreciative.

To my parents and my sister, thank you for believing in me. Always.